ALPHABET
OF THE NIGHT

JEAN-EUPHÈLE MILCÉ

ALPHABET
OF THE NIGHT

Translated from the French
by Christopher Moncrieff

PUSHKIN PRESS
LONDON

For Caroline, again with much gratitude

English translation © Christopher Moncrieff 2007

First published in French as
L'Alphabet des nuits © Bernard Campiche Editeur 2004

This edition first published in 2007 by
Pushkin Press
12 Chester Terrace
London N1 4ND

British Library Cataloguing in Publication Data:
A catalogue record for this book is available
from the British Library

ISBN (13) 978 1 901285 76 5
ISBN (10) 1 901285 76 6

Cover: *Voodoo Haiti* 2003
© Tiane Doan na Champassak/Agence VU

Frontispiece: Jean-Euphèle Milcé
© Horst Tappe

Set in 10½ on 13½ Monotype Baskerville
and printed in Great Britain
by TJ International, Padstow, Cornwall

This book is supported by the French Ministry of Foreign Affairs, as part
of the Burgess Programme run by the Cultural Department of the French
Embassy in London.

Liberté • Égalité • Fraternité
RÉPUBLIQUE FRANÇAISE

*Ouvrage publié avec le concours du
Ministère Français chargé de la culture—Centre national du Livre*

To a child who might be called Sébastien, Juliane, Chrystelle, Réginald, Océane, Each time the family's dusty footsteps tell the story of the crossing.

For Carmen Milcé, Daniel Gombau, Laura Saggiorato, Jean-Marc Maradan, Michel Lebrun.

Increase our taxes, ask us for much gold and silver, for a Jew will give all he possesses for his country.

RABBI ISAAC ABRAVANEL

PART ONE

1

THE DAWN BRINGS ME its first tints in changing swirls of colour. Port-au-Prince always wakes to find its cries, its ill-expressed sorrows smothered by a pall of smoke. Rising up from the ground, hopes destroyed by the daily struggle for survival hang over a place that has lost all sense of being a capital. The town howls. Its voice fills the air along with the shouts of the thousands of street vendors, the bootblacks, those polishers of oppressive boots. As if we have been under constant shellfire, smoke rises straight into the sky, blocking out the light. It is the omen of another dreary day.

I warm up last night's coffee. Everything that finds its way through the darkness of this country holds within itself a shred of memory, a little cache of lost lives. How can you do business in a country where nothing is stable? Every day brings new prices, new things forgotten. Damn it all! Who can tell me what happened last night? We are all accessories to the silence, to the night's ghostly patrol car made of matchboxes.

Lucien will be here any minute. To the customers he is the security guard. But the fact is, he knows the shop needs him and his sawn-off Winchester. His job is to prove we are not secure. To me he is an employee, a friend, a passive lover. Every morning he comes into my bedroom, brushes against my senses, takes down the old shotgun then wanders off to drink the hot rum that helps him play the part of a security guard.

Time to open the shop. I take the ton of padlocks off the door. The air doesn't smell good today. It is the same breeze that brought the news that my cousin had been found dead without her jewels. It is that silent gust of wind which brings out the town's rage, blurs the boundaries of what is imaginable. Padlock by padlock, word after word.

Lucien is not superstitious. He is simply afraid of the dark at high noon. He acts as a shield for a washed-out business that keeps on losing its customers. Every week I count up the missing and the dead. I even like to think I am up to date. Joël has left. Mariette has lost her job. Fritz has been executed. No one dared die a natural death.

It is eight o'clock on a shipwrecked morning, wrinkled, scorched by exhaustion. Lucien is at his post outside the door, ready for the long ritual. Without him, what is left of my customers would not come and buy condensed milk, sugar, boxes of anti-mosquito spirals, cheese, flour. I am scared. The security Lucien provides is small-scale. People believe he can use that gun they all see. But he is just absorbed in his games. Every day he bets a glass of *tafia* that he will come home safe. The rough alcohol is eating away at his lungs. He coughs to show that he is still alive. And when he thinks he has a reason to be doubly alive, he increases the dose and collapses, delirious.

Lucien's nights are filled with his plans from the daytime. He knows the four o'clock news always gives the latest number of dead. Anyone could be on the list. Security guards first and foremost. But his fight for survival does not give him time to work out what the metaphor for the end might be. Every day could be the end of a world or the end of a man. To hide is suicide, to live merely dangerous. This town would be dead even without the poverty that drives people to attack the Place de la Cathédrale, the seashore and anywhere in between. There is no doubt about it, my shop makes a living off those who have departed and those who plan to depart. A drop of water for Georges, a pinch of salt for Clara, a nip of three-star Barbancourt rum for Simon and Jacques. In the name of all those who have left, rightly or wrongly, and who are watching us from the great unknown, I declare my day open.

The first customer who comes to the till hands over his money with the first news of the day:

"More than a thousand homes were destroyed last night in a fire at Varreux. Residents claim they caught workers from the National Electricity Company pouring fuel oil into the large stagnant canal that runs through the shanty town. They then got a fire going, making people run for their lives and killing mosquitoes, dogs, children and the elderly. The strongest tried to contain the blaze. But they couldn't. Everyone resigned themselves. We are so used to living with the living dead that all we can do is tighten our belts yet again. The pain is gut-wrenching. If life came back with every new day, we wouldn't give a damn about the dead; but, poor devils that we are, all we have left are memories."

It is the season for nonsense, open to exile. Another customer arrives. She doesn't even do me the honour of looking at me. I assume she is hiding the clouds of the night. The silence of the morning is another sign of the nightmares people live. Warily she looks at the shelves. It is as if there was a ghost in every tin of food. Her footsteps scrape the floorboards, accompanied by the sound of her chattering teeth. Her fear is the same as everyone else's. An everyday fear, easily recognised. Being a good salesman I show her my haggard face. My real face. At the till she will take at least five minutes to jam her purse back down inside her bra.

"Drivers of public transport are threatening to strike in protest against armed fare-dodgers. This is the fifth such action in the space of a

month. The public transport drivers' main demand is directed towards a substantial drop in the price of oil products. There is no need to point out that this sector is of vital importance for the daily life of the country. Members of the public are already worried about a slowdown in their businesses if no agreement is reached between the parties concerned within the next twenty-four hours."

The news breaks in little flakes. This latest broadcast comes from the channel run by the current opposition party.

2

THE STREET TAKES ON its colours, despite the expectation of a day of mourning. To me, every day is much the same. I've seen so many. Tomorrow's costumes are not in my diary. It's not my problem. Habits are like gangrene. They get into your bones, go with you to the grave. I admit there are little things I am fond of. Starting the day without them is like an old wound that has faded. You find yourself rubbing the scar to get the last drop of pus.

Lucien's favourite street-seller should be here soon. It is five years since she took over the job from her mother, who died in a sanatorium from a bad case of tuberculosis. For five years she has not grown. She has just kept the wrinkles from her crumpled adolescence. If she didn't have this job, she would probably be a beggar or a whore. Being a whore is a more serious business. It allows you to be out late at night, gives you a grandstand view. There are so many things to see in this country. Hookers are part of the scenery of the night. They have a multiple visa up their skirts.

But the street-seller prefers the daytime game. She is even pale. Basket on her head, she goes round selling her smoked herring pasta and hard-boiled eggs. She provides Lucien with his lunch. I love to see him, gun across his knees, sniffing her pasta. She always serves it to him on a white enamel plate. It is Lucien's plate. I am rather jealous of the pasta-seller's voice, her long blue skirt and red sandals. Poor Lucien: he can't chat people up while I'm around. We have a pact. I told him that our relationship is sustained by a mutual need to barricade up our fate and ward off our fears. I would like to see him wake up every morning with a woman who cooks pasta for him and brings him his coffee. I have never had that sort of life; and I admit it doesn't feature among my interests.

On both sides of the road, shop windows unveil their take-away dreams. In this neighbourhood, business is not done in a conventional way. We all understand each other. We work together. People buy things in bulk from me then sell them on just outside my shop. To an outsider it might seem an odd way of working, unfair competition. But we have our code of practice in the unofficial market, the underground. I am a fully paid-up member of this family of hawkers, of satis-fiers-of-hunger. It is the strangers that frighten us. Even in the middle of the dense, thronging crowds you can recognise a newcomer by getting a sense of his intentions.

The girl, the pasta-seller, comes into the shop with her blue skirt, her red sandals, but without her basket. She looks seri-ous. Her breasts are almost bursting out of her blouse. She leans right up against the counter and says:

"Monsieur Assaël, I've just been serving Police Constable Gaspard. He was in a hurry to finish eating because he's on official business. He's waiting for a colleague who's got a score to settle with a security guard. You know, Monsieur Assaël, security guards, there's a lot round here. But I know them all. The police officer didn't say much. But his vague description reminded me of Lucien. I think the other police-man has got a grudge against this security guard, who insulted him in a bar when he wasn't in uniform. Please, do something for my customer. My instinct tells me it's him. Ask him to come inside, hide him. Heaven will reward you many times over."

I come out from behind the counter. Let's call it an attempt. The thunderbolt had time to rip up the street-seller's bid to intervene and to shatter my memory. The gunshot was close. Too close. Lucien is dead.

Lucien died as he lived: without joy. I have a feeling my life is going to plunge into the communal grave. The policeman who had a grudge against Lucien did not even bother to hide. He did not come into the shop. He had obviously finished his day's work; or it was just an extension of his night.

I left the door open with Lucien lying across it. The Rue du Commerce has succeeded in driving me out. Me, the third generation of Assaëls in Haiti, and I am being forced to run away. My family has lived in this country since the time of the generals on horseback at the four gates of the capital. There is no such thing as a Jew without a shop in any of the Banana Republics. It is our sector, our means of survival; the only real connection we have with these countries.

3

CURFEW IN MY HEAD. It is the same all the time here, in this country that has always lived in me. I can't move. Close the shop. Drink the last glass of rum. Leave. This country is pursuing me. It takes its siesta at the same time as me. We are both failures, caught by a ravaged, ragged history. And my future? Where is it trapped? I was born of imported parents, with no land of my own.

I dream of a life where you don't wake up with the taste of sulphur in your mouth, where you aren't surrounded by empty cartridges and the tell-tale marks of machetes. I am losing my customers. Alice has gone up north somewhere. Jeannine is still lying low in some embassy, waiting to get her marching orders through the back door of the Interior Ministry. Apparently her husband has been reported missing since a price was put on his head. Jeannine is swimming with all she has left of her flesh and blood, despairing at the uncertain tomorrows. Her daughter, who used to ask me for Swiss chocolate on the sly, managed to make the fraternity of killers exhaust themselves with pleasure. Her body was covered in bruises, her sex full of answers and injuries. Lucien's body is still lying outside the door in a pool of blood.

And that is how every awakening goes down in history, how it returns to the annals of time, those guardians of outdated bric-a-brac. Headless lives. Hopes dismantled in a hurry.

Still, you get used to being alive. God damn it! Won't a flash of lightning penetrate my sober sense of reason? I can't find enough paper to swallow up my Jewish roots. I am in transit in a displaced country lost at sea. I claim to associate a piece of stumbling, badly-played jazz with every friend of mine who is missing. I don't ask to live in an area where I have ties. Yet my shop is a place for selling, bartering, for political down-and-outs. Unlike the other shopkeepers I know, I choose to listen to my customers.

I have always been fond of this kind of work: a counter, plenty of faces coming and going, whining, puffed up with their own importance. With my ethnic background I could never have been a psychologist.

Port-au-Prince's awakenings sing of wounds inflicted on the sun. Each morning it picks up one less spear. I don't wish to play the prophet in a country that belongs to the wild laughter of rapists, but I foresee an eternal eclipse before the end of my world. To live here is to accept the burden of Lucien's death. It is to accept that you have to castrate your own words. Like the cry of the waves on a stormy night, the people come out of their cardboard city, out of its courtyards that wear the colours of another life, to launch an attack on the town. We know that without rumours, without courtyards full of traps, Port-au-Prince would be unable to find its footing as the town of the ogre, the manager of illusions smothered during the birth of desires.

Every crossroads is willing to listen to passions that are dead and gone. They are washed regularly by floods caused by the horror that sweeps away anything that shows signs of taking root, leaving behind dreams of victories won by loyalty. And just so no one is in any doubt, this city's tortured crossroads start to panic if you stare at them too long. By order of the dynasty of big chiefs, anything that stays here longer than a season is accused of plotting against the security of the destructive order. Out of habit, and respect for today's movers and shakers, Port-au-Prince has been declared a transit town.

I ask myself why I waited until I saw Lucien's lifeless body before deciding to break with destiny. Perhaps, like the missionary Johnny Bell, I was dreaming of the steep climb to redemption. Every time he tries to convert me to Protestant Christianity, all he talks about is the town being cursed. According to him, God chose this town to test out his concept of Hell. People who live here get the best education there is in fighting against pain and evil.

It is not by chance that the missions and congregations randomly offload all their deviants onto this city's welcoming shores. That is why you meet paedophile headmasters, swindlers in charge of humanitarian aid, Nazi prison chaplains. Sometimes the words of Bell the missionary fill the space in my drifting hopes. Today more than ever I want to believe his theory, that this town is Hell's laboratory. I am going to answer the call of the underground. I have fought it for too long.

4

THE SEAL OF POLICE officer Amazan on a stamped piece of paper, which has to be paid for first, is the last obstacle before gaining access to the main street of Gonaïves, my family's first adopted town.

Along a weary old road that reminds you of the chaos you find after a place has been cleared of mines, you enter the little town of salt marshes. The houses, leaning against posts eaten away by the salt, almost buried in dust, preside over a deathbed scene. During daylight the cathedral, closely protected by its parade ground or the heroes of the Independence, meets the eye from all directions. This iconic landmark of the town has never changed; it must hide the secret of how the game is played. Endlessly.

I spent the first twelve years of my life in this town, which prolongs the status of *moun vini,** strangers who arrived in cardboard boxes. This is no longer a secret. Jews, Levantines and other white folk are the first boat people Haiti can remember. Well might the history books talk about the Italian navigator who led a horde of subjects belonging to Her Very Catholic Majesty the Queen of Spain; people don't give a damn. That's all in the past. Nonetheless, the island has known others: little French Whites, enlisted men, black

---

* Foreigners.

merchandise dumped in the plantations, penniless Germans from grimy Hamburg, surplus Italians from New York's overflow. Everyone has been here. Yet despite the colour of their skin, Jews and other Levantines are regarded differently. We marry among ourselves and enlarge our shops.

The dusty serenity of Gonaïves catches me in the throat. As a child I wanted to claim I belonged here. My family made it their solemn duty to see that I did not form any lasting attachment to the place. Their lives were spent waiting for a promised land somewhere in the world. Despite the existence of the State of Israel, my family kept putting down roots along the road. And I have no right to get other ideas. But it does not alter the fact that we have been here for almost a century, that I have played football on all the town's makeshift pitches that haven't been ruined. More and more I get the impression of having entered the adult world while closing the door on my childhood. My years of belonging *de facto* to a community of children swarming through the peaceful main streets have no connection with the reality of being a shopkeeper on holiday accidentally, although technically out-of-work.

The same day
1 p m

I stop at Chez Frantz.

I almost missed the door of the restaurant. I like this place. It would have been a pity to walk straight past. Such absent-mindedness would have forced me to ask directions from the locals, to retrace my steps, to walk back over two kilometres of potholed roads. I came back here two years ago, to get revenge on desires of mine which have been lost over the years. My friends and I were impressed by what this restaurant represented for us. It haunted our youth. Every Friday afternoon we used to come to the Avenue des Dattes to steal sugar cane. We never left before the start of the Rotary Club meeting. To begin the meeting, the Club members had to sing a verse from the national anthem: *"For the flag, for the homeland, let us dig with joy."*

I never saw anyone from my family at this meeting of worthies. My father always lied to me about it. He told me he was not invited for several reasons, such as the Rotarians' habit of hitting the bottle. He likened their meetings to drinking sessions. It was not that he couldn't afford the subscription, or that he wasn't pale enough. What he failed to tell me was that he was a banished White, of doubtful stock. He knew that the other Whites did not have to slave away in order to earn a living. They are part and parcel of the plan to whiten the race. That is why they can marry the children of politicians to produce mulattos. These breeders have access to all levels of government, to all the clubs. Unlike us, these invaders only set foot in dearest Haiti with the idea of making a life for themselves. They have run away from unemployment, legal proceedings, hypocrisy. My parents were not that kind of casual displaced person. I am from the people of no fixed abode.

The restaurant Chez Frantz has lost yet another star. The last time I came I imagined I was taking away two. Legitimate revenge. The Rotary Club has completely disintegrated. A victim of prudent exiles. The national anthem is never sung now, only played. Monsieur Esdras has been Club President for over ten years. He comes out of habit, like a sleepwalker at the waning moon. At the start of each meeting he pours a glass of Coke for every permanent absentee. He has stopped paying his subscription. Besides, there is no longer a fund. The wife of the last treasurer handed it all over to the colonel to pay for her husband's tuberculosis treatment in prison.

The Rotary Club now only exists in memories. A few diehard members still dare get together. It is their way of recovering from careers cut short, the pain of life after prison, businesses seized because of colleagues who headed for the hills. No more worthies, just the salt breeze that blows on the outskirts of a new neighbourhood.

I am too bitter to notice the relentless call of the hummingbird in the flowers on the balcony. It seems his ancestors always did the same thing at the same time. Perhaps this one came back with damaged wings, or with the pain of his fellow creatures that fell during the journey. But he did not take the time to make friends again with the place that once sheltered him as a station on the route of his life. I had to stumble over the image of Lucien's body dripping with blood before I could understand the eternal, unchanging flight of the hummingbird.

I am not a fugitive. No complaints have been made about me. Lucien's body is already in the communal grave that is avoided even by Baron la Croix, who handles the mysteries of life in death. I am not going to be a witness. I'd rather close my shop. But the news is spreading across the *département*. The domineering and excessive voice of the Republic of Port-au-Prince imposes itself on the other Haiti:

"The President of the Republic has called an urgent meeting of the Chiefs of Police of the country's nine geographic départements. The schedule for this meeting, planned for tomorrow at the National Palace, has been published by the presidential press bureau. On the agenda will be the opening of a debate on the latest outbreak of violent robberies that are threatening the credibility of the revolutionary government. The Head of State has made it clear that he fought his election campaign on the issues of security, economic growth and social justice. He has every intention of working with the government to achieve results that are in line with the promises he made. The death toll from last night is twelve."

Without pausing for breath, the presenter moves on to the rest of the news.

"Shopkeepers from this country have moved their businesses to the Dominican Republic. To help them set up, the Dominican authorities have given them substantial tax relief and aids to integration. At a press conference in the Dominican capital this morning, according to a report by the government press agency, these stateless people spoke of the climate of fear in Haiti, and the burdens imposed by the country's administration. Apparently they left the country owing ten year's unpaid tax."

5

MUSIC FILLS THE CAR. I have no desire to get out. Too tired. My immediate plan is to rediscover a particular corner in the playground of the École des Frères, a school for Christian education. I let my portable cassette player keep playing. For me, each missing friend has their own few bars of music. Today I am listening for Fresnel. We grew up together. It was with him I marked out all the doorways in this part of town, which has changed so little over the years. When we needed to, we came here to hide to escape punishment. We kissed each other dozens of times, because we were children, because it was habit. One day he said it was better cuddling me than being subjected to Brother Pascal's bad breath.

We spent most of our time spitting out the taste of cheap tobacco and fear after having to pay another visit to the office of our cassock-wearing instructor. Over the years our love created affection and complicity between us. But it was nothing compared to the power of a counsellor that the Brother, our teacher and lover, was always imparting to us.

I haven't heard from Fresnel for days. I can't imagine he has disappeared in the wild frenzy of a night from which there is no return. Maybe they haven't had time to take him to prison yet. Killed on the spot by mistake. I always thought he would come to a tragic end. He drinks too much, and with anybody. He's crazy when he's drunk, just blurts things out.

The militia are everywhere, listening. No one knows who is going to inform on who. When flies are in the air, you can't tell what sex they are. And this is definitely a state of flies. They poison everything, do it with a passion.

Once again the idea of death has just passed through my life. Always in the same direction. It would be insensitive to talk about coincidence, about victims who never stood a chance. Even in my head, blues music is redesigning the eternity of tastes. I know it would please Fresnel, the artist of absence. I invest this place of our forbidden games with the fear that I will invent a way of managing departures. First him, and then Lucien. My relationship with Fresnel began when I found a reason to love, to give myself. As for Lucien, he was a passing affair that lasted. We made love out of solidarity, out of a need to make the most of the rare mornings we were given.

Music is a cure for fear. It has countless lives. I always buy two of the same record. I listen to them. I copy them on disc. I put them on cassette. On Sundays I used to go and listen to old records at Fresnel's place. I liked his little house at Pétion-Ville, his way of associating music with our every gesture. We always made love to a background of *a cappella*. Once he was satisfied, he often left me in bed with the smell of our bodies to go for a drink and talk history with his fellow teachers. He knew more about my family than my father did. Other people's histories are his passion. He only has me and a few friends he once spent a night with who will have experienced the intimacy of rare moments that are totally his, without any history, without the need to prove anything to others.

According to the rumours, we were blood brothers, baptised together, business associates, old friends, but never lovers. It is true we were already adolescents when we arrived in the capital with the same recommendations from Brother Pascal for the Little Seminary of the Collège Saint-Martial. People saw us arrive. I am a white Jew, the son of a provincial grocer. Fresnel is a mulatto from the same place. These outward signs blocked access to my nudity. As long as this country has amnesia, my past is protected. People pass through, stopping just long enough to shatter their lives on the pylons of the town, whose length is forever unknown. Around me grows the time of a solitary past. Not a single old person remembers me growing up. Nobody wants to remember anything. The past is left to drift away in the mists of dawn. Without descendants, without a prayer. You are alone with destiny, the destiny of someone who is just passing through.

I have no more school friends left. They are all dead; or worse, they have left. The last one who called in at the shop to say hello thought I looked old and shabby. He had trouble finding a safe Western product without too much fat content. I thought he was a bit too obsessive about the nasty little bacteria we eat here from morning 'til night. He normally did his shopping at the big, sterile supermarket chains. He left the way he came: as a tourist.

He reminded me of my years with the Brothers at the school for Christian education. It was a socialisation project whose secret was known only to my father. My native community seems to have a divine mission to colonise. It always joins the most reactionary local movement, the one closest to the powers that be. Like a long-term investment I found myself placed among the legal Whites of this country. The Brother-Headmaster only accepted me after making my father promise that I would not be allowed to run rackets with my classmates, selling them trinkets and broken biscuits.

I hear the six o'clock news over the twelve rows of bricks round what used to be my school, where you learnt everything, even how to love in a good non-Christian way.

"American coastal patrols have picked up what remains of a boat—two hundred and six passengers, including crew—which had most likely sunk in the Vent Canal. To date, American figures, which are reliable, show that more than two million people have braved sea crossings to get to the coast of Florida. Are they fleeing poverty or terror? Of these latter-day adventurers, five hundred thousand have managed to get through the protective wire fencing along the coast. Two hundred thousand have been turned back to Haiti and the rest unfortunately perished. Of those turned back to Haiti, half have already disappeared. Twenty thousand of them are clinically insane. At night they can be heard telling the story of the struggle of their hopes against the cynicism of the waves."

And the news continues:

"Former Police Inspector Paul Jumelot was arrested this morning for conspiracy against State security. He has been taken under close surveillance to a secret location known only to the Bureau for Investigation and Action for Internal Security."

6

THE FLEETING CRIES of nightfall glance off the final notes of a treacly performance of blues, muffled and slow-moving. The imaginary presence of Fresnel drifts around in the growing darkness, leaving brief reflections of our first acts of madness that were really just *faux pas*. It is the moment to let myself be absorbed by the hesitation of our bodies parted for ever, by the uncontrolled echoes of our elation. In the death pangs of each minute that carries off the remains of the sun into the depths of the night, my rootless mind withdraws to the ruins of my loves, to the bundle that is Lucien, his blood, into the finality of a vanished word.

The day, the physical symbol of flourishing life, disappears with its knapsack still undone. Out of it tumbles a ray of sunshine, the last chime of the ice-cream man's bell, the furtive bouncing of a ball, a last display of kites tearing holes in the north wind. The people of Gonaïves get ready to greet the night. The town has no choice but to obey the wishes of the darkness. No one knows if the neighbourhoods that have trouble lighting up are not part of some mysterious plan to stop life going on. In my little corner, Fresnel's reawakened tenderness seeps into my pores, places a kiss in my path. But the weight of the dead who lie submerged in my fear suddenly comes to the surface. A desire to take my rips and tears into the first all-night bar I come to along my broken road.

The town catches up with me once I get to the power station. All night its roaring will be in the ears of the people who live nearby. None of them like to go to bed without this accompaniment. The ten big petrol engines keep on running, providing the tempo for the right to exist. I am going to attack the town at the part that is hidden from the inquisition. I too have the right to wear a mask of normality, to feed off the habit of dying. The car will take me through the streets of the little town, past houses almost buried like drowned dreams during the last rains. At ten kilometres-an-hour, with muted movements, like the winding spiral of men and women with a naked destiny, my mind will unwind in a wave of taboos.

At the door of the Café du Port the precocious night breeze dies away. My family knew this town during the time of the bogeymen. My parents always discouraged me from coming here. It is an area that has never been built up, but which grew to serve the needs of ship-owners searching for love, shifty-looking soldiers, writers without family ties, good-time girls whose lace gets excited by the mist. This is the place to come for everyday slap-and-tickle. It is forbidden to talk of sadness here. Everyone parades their own particular reason for living, puts their cards on the table. The aim of the non-stop music is to fill the room with shrill, lively, tropical notes. No one has the decency, let alone the strength to keep still.

Like an anthill at harvest time, footsteps take bodies, tired but happy, from tables to the bar, from the bar to the dance floor, from the dance floor to the bedroom and from the bedroom to seventh heaven.

Pleasure has been decreed a substitute for conscience, a painkiller for misfortune. Even when happiness is writ large in the subdued light, every creaking door adds a strangled voice to the necklace of stolen lives. Wounds, concealed by the attitude of girls who rule over nights behind closed doors, get a cynical reception. Queens of the night, witches of the day, they live in fear of dawn's approach. The daylight likes to feed on make-up and illicit perfume. No one is sole owner of the non-stop party. The prostitutes at the harbour turn their backs on the sun and look forward to the reign of the half-light.

I have just discovered the many-headed spectacle of unconditional love. The woman who owns the bar has a sales technique quite unlike my own. To work at this counter you mustn't be inquisitive. Above all you have to know how to corrupt every client who arrives by chance or in need of therapy. I am too sad to be any good at selling fantasies. I always try and find an echo of the street in people's gestures. Sometimes, in the eyes of an upper-crust woman, I manage to understand her fear of a night of vampires. As a rule I am interested in my customers' wounds. I am an inquisitive sales-man; along with my passions, my special offers, my everyday products, I go into all the houses in the area. My clients see me in my shop calendar pinned up on their living-room wall. Perhaps they see me in the Sacred Heart of Jesus, printed by the thousand at the end of December, in every promise of a national holiday.

Never has there been such a total ban on rumours from outside. The news bounces off the armour plating of the cursed and happy harbour district. One after another the queens come walking along their patch, disappearing behind a door into places big enough for two. It is a good idea to have a drink. It is advisable to make love. It is wise to forget your sorrows. The news will wait outside the door for morn-ing. This special neighbourhood beside the sea is deaf, and suffers from amnesia.

7

MORNING FOUND ME down at the harbour, by a sea that was pursuing an old, everyday wave. It caught me with my head in hands that were still warm with desire. Its rhythm stood bolt upright in my path. I have a horror of the sea. It is too closely linked to my family history. How many Jews have made a destiny for themselves out of fantasies about the ocean swell? I have no right to leave. The sea reminds me too much of running away, of stories told to one horizon after another. My family tradition is a bottle thrown by a chain of events, trailing behind it a stream of discriminations crammed together in every harbour in the world.

Instinctively I step back from the sea. How can a whole race make an entry in their diary which might involve being tossed about by floods? To my way of thinking, exile is that profound self-perception that comes after every journey into the events and places nearest me.

Permanent escape. This is the sum total of my inheritance. It is more than a century since my family settled in this country, juggling their shop with the bureaucracy of consumer regulations, and already I want to leave; and that is the best reason of all. In one of his escapist, Sunday moods, Fresnel suggested I do a survey of the twenty-eight thousand square kilometres that make up this country. I always treated his suggestions like just another product on offer, of no interest to a good businessman. I always frustrated his efforts to introduce me to anything apart from my shop and our Sundays of love. Now I see how pitiful I am to rely on rumours, on what others tell me. And what others?

I grew up wedged between two shelves. At home we had a swimming pool, built to make my father's last days more comfortable. Most of the time it was empty, due to lack of water and guests. I never benefited from this luxury to wash away the traces of ludicrous, irrational games (to use my father's expression). The sound of celebrations and holidays fell flat at home. They were always kept indoors to be corrected. Before letting them out again, our way of life took care to prune out any heathen songs, the music of sloth. This is where I get my fear of taking time, of seeing the other world. It contrasts amazingly with my desire to sin; or, to put it nicely, to finish the apple that Adam could never eat while he was under the malicious gaze of the Creator.

A young boy crosses the road without looking. A butterfly chases him and his madness. It appears he comes down to the harbour every morning to bunk off school, and to avoid the spoonful of cod liver oil that, here in the north, they give to the scrawny, delicate kids from the south. Every morning he follows the same instinct, a child wound up in his wounds.

The radio is intrusive. It yells. It is an all-purpose machine. No one dares wake up without it. The radio drives away the night and forecasts the colours of the day. For over ten years, no one has dared go out or send their children to school without getting the go-ahead from the radio. It punctuates the day with its advertising jungles. It entertains. It distracts. Scattered over gullible ears glued to it expectantly, today's news is interwoven with that of yesterday and the day before, like a roll of film that rewinds itself in blood after a tasteless show. You could not say that the radio uses the language of madness and grief deliberately. Politics and fate have already killed off the time of appeasement.

Who can tell me when in the history of this place the streets rid themselves of the lunatics who used to go round everywhere, hugging the walls and putting up posters of the current heads to be cut off or stuck back on? The tropics and the devastating hurricanes will have to die out before the tide of fear goes down. We Jews, who ransack the land without ever working it, have never invented a new language. We have been content to cover the town with our stalls, remaining silent and unmoving in the face of bad customers. The people's militia may be right to leave misunderstood, simple and absent-minded crimes outside the door of our shops and homes. We came from far away to build a republic of clients. Our principle is to be at their disposal, to quicken the drug effect that our shelves have on them. It has always worked because the Revolution has never been so accurate, so targeted.

We have always believed that the politics of the national palace regularly renews itself, leaving needs and desires unchanged. In our most fearful dreams, this era has not revealed the most obscure aspect of its face. I belong to this community, one which is suffering a dramatic loss of power.

I am the unworthy heir of a line of merchants. I regret that I am not up to the job of maintaining the well-established family firm. I closed the shop before having the electronic signboard put up across the front. It is true that the power has been cut off for a long time, and the little generator can't handle any more, but I should have invested in another source of power. Then my name would have been picked up by every pair of eyes, spread all over town, discussed in every home, creating a desire for the shop to reopen. But I think I have become a sad case, keener to campaign for love than for memories.

At school with Fresnel, in this my town of refuge, there was reading aloud, gold stars in our report books to encourage us. I spent the first twelve years of my life with a head full of subconscious dreams. The harbour, the streets as straight as the letter 'I', the abandoned lighthouse, are as much a weight as a way of not forgetting. Adult life transformed the little bell of my games—most of them forbidden—into a muffled roar that means rebellion or permanent exile. I came back to this town to cry tears of anxiety, to lessen Fresnel's absence under the microscope of memories. I am afraid I will forget how to untie the knot of our passion. I am now certain that my debt to him is clearer and more exacting than the debt to my family. I am going to come back from the dead, starting from this town that sketched the outlines of an alliance of heart and sense.

> *"Reactions from all of Haiti's political class in exile, and even those of some foreign governments and personalities, keep coming in to our editorial offices after the shocking assassination of Father Jacques Lachenet. Through its official nunciature in Haiti, the Vatican has made a vehement protest against the impunity enjoyed by criminals. It is particularly worried about the tendency to trivialise crime in a Christian country. There is no need to remind you that Father Lachenet is well known throughout Latin America for his stand in favour of preaching reparation. He is leader of a movement that accuses the Church of encouraging and taking part in colonisation, of having supported plans for the impoverishment and loss of dignity of the native populations of America and of those who came from Africa. We find the Vatican's open letter surprising, given the reluctance of the Holy Father to support the late priest's theological masturbation—to use the words of the Archbishop. But there is no need for alarm. An inquiry has been opened and will continue indefinitely."*

This piece of news exposes the presenter's own fears. He is usually so careful about the tone he uses, depending on where the sun is in the sky and on advertising contracts. I once persuaded him to promote a new brand of razors for me. He presented my product as if it was a weapon against man-eating beards. Everyone believed him; sales figures far exceeded all my expectations.

8

I REALISE THAT FATHER LACHENET was an important person.
I had to put up with him for six years of my adolescence at
the Collège Saint-Martial. I didn't really like him. But in this
turmoil of words, deaths and bankrupt hopes, you hang on to,
cling on to, graft yourself onto every pain. Perhaps it is the time
for solidarity, for the reverse side of the seasons.

The first time I met the late priest was the day I took
my entrance exam for the Collège Saint-Martial, a school
renowned for its expertise in helping revive the country's
elite. However stupid a politician might be, somewhere on
his curriculum vitae he has a few years at this expensive,
prestigious and austere school. Concentrating on the questions on my commentary sheet, I tried to avoid the presence
of this Father who watched me throughout the test. When
I handed in my script, he stared at me for a long time with
eyes that were devoid of feeling. I realised that never again
would I find a religious ear to listen to the song of my restless
nights. No more holy hands on my child's skin. The time of
memories was fast approaching. I felt deposed, deprived of
my privileges.

For four whole years I was never able to get close to Father
Lachenet. At the end of each year he came to give out the
annual reports. He always held mine between his finger and
thumb and looked at it for three or four minutes. He was

interested in my results. I never was. Sometimes I heard him laughing in the library, where every afternoon he shut himself away with young people from the *collège* and the *lycées* in the town. I imagined him spending his life writing forewords for the plans of his friends' lives. I was still not in his group. But I sensed my day was coming. He did not mix with the babies of the *collège*. His thing was the big boys.

In the October when I went into the Humanities class, he was appointed to the tenure of Haitian History. I found myself in the front row, in a seating plan he had drawn up himself. He called all the pupils by their first name, except me. Yet I was one of the rare Whites—and thus visible—in a class that was mostly black or mulatto. My family was not unknown, although not highly thought of in political and intellectual circles. But although we lived modestly, no one could accuse us of being poor. Not content with just paying my school fees, my family contributed to the cost of all the extracurricular activities. I was a good pupil. My love affair with Fresnel was now ten years old. Despite the hotheadedness and desires of our adolescence, we had never openly publicised our relationship. Our secret had the advantage of putting distance between us and the school, through the magic of our journeys to celebrate our childhood, intact and restored to our games.

In a few months, the Father-Incumbent got me to visit places connected with the history of families like mine, something I had always refrained from doing, even with good analytical tools. He had the words for, and a way of talking about the all-pervasive Jews, who do not have any popular, proletarian project in mind. At first I took him for a dreamer who, instead of keeping his feet on the ground was trying to blow it up, to the detriment of anyone trying to hang on. I did not feel the least bit guilty about having an immigrant Jew for a father. I knew this country had been looted from the moment it appeared in the history books. Spaniards, English, French, their sons calling themselves Haitians, Germans, Italians, Black Americans, Levantines, Jews: they had all passed through. The Black Africans who think they belong here are not the first arrivals. Haiti is an open country, a mosaic.

In my reasoning and my personal situation, I used these rational words to fill the emptiness left by the arrows that the Father fired during history lessons. I had to react in public in order to ring my little bell, the victim's bell. In the playground, like attracted like. But I was not like anyone. Even Fresnel had found other interests. People only came to me to set up a fund to pay for the sharing-out of gifts at the end-of-term prize-giving or other celebrations.

Father Lachenet never came into the playground, but in his absence I felt his presence. I heard him everywhere, in the whispering, when others ran away. Two weeks after my declaration of principles— which he found rather pompous—he called me into his office, a colourless box collapsing under the weight of books two centuries older than him—or that was how it seemed—to confess something to me. He began by asking me to leave the school voluntarily. According to him, a well-educated Jew is a threat to future generations. And in the end, Haiti has to become a nation. This is very complex, with all the various groups who have different-coloured skin as well as different economic situations. The case of the Jews could be even more difficult. They have no real roots. Their memory is confined to their business to start with; and since time immemorial, the moment they become rich they expand and demand the right of ascendancy over all the peoples of the world. They believe they are God's direct descendents. And since the earth and all it contains belongs to God, it follows that the Jews, who are God's heirs, should claim to be owner-managers of the earth, and especially its wealth.

His speech left me with no choice. My father helped me understand the political class's need for nationalism in the direction they had taken. I knew our role was to provide the people here with cheap rubbish and goods from the rest of the world, while still getting them to dream. With our seeming success, we had to take hold of people by their belly and their desires. For their part, they would carry on with politics and come to us at the appropriate time, such as for financing an election campaign against the promise of franchises.

The following year I left the *collège* and went to study accountancy in the United States. I wanted to go to university and then teach. Alas: the destiny of every Jew leads him to the back room of a shop.

Not long afterwards, on the *Voice of America* programme, I heard that Father Lachenet had been arrested and forced into exile:

"A communiqué from the press-relations department of the Ministry of Foreign Affairs and Religious Worship has published the names of members of religious orders who have been declared persona non grata on Haitian territory. These priests were running a network of young leftists without patriotic sympathies. The government, which is mindful of respecting the Constitution, upholds people's rights of association; but it also has a duty to ensure that the country's future decision-makers get a good education. It is with the aim of protecting the student community that the police have been ordered to break up this network which, in its way of operating, had every appearance of a breeding ground for terrorists. Subversive books and leaflets have been seized and destroyed. Father Lachenet, the main instigator of this movement, has been stripped of Haitian nationality and banned for life from living on Haitian territory."

When there was a change of those in power, Father Lachenet naturally came back. He rediscovered the good intentions of his militant tendency. This grieved me, but I understood his position.

9

1st November

2 30 p m

LESS THAN TEN KILOMETRES to go before Port-au-Prince gets to me. The city is well protected by rows of shanty towns with a line of cracks down the middle. Port-au-Prince is the sort of capital that anticipates your intentions. The town never lets itself be caught out. I am one of those who come back to rake over the ashes, to refresh the blood. Murderous twinges grip my heart. I worry about my many different survival instincts, which obscure any sensitive impulse, the right to be human. Most of all I am mesmerised by the military activity, the searching looks, the menacing talk of the poor people which bombard me whenever I stop. The mere idea of the smell of the streets, the whispering of the haggard houses, the weight of the voices, makes me hide behind my salesman's vigilance on the main road to Port-au-Prince, a road which is crumbling, at the end of its tether.

I have got older just thinking about skirting round the town and its rhythms on the edge of the darkness. Common sense reels around on my suppressed sobs. Why did I choose All Souls' Day, the procession of the *guédés*, to take a road that struggles towards my return? I left this place under a deluge of alarming news. The traffic defies time and any urban logic. From all directions, the dance is approaching. It is a road in the shape of a cross, lost in the cemetery. My patience opens like a tomb the council has ordered to be reused. Among my most recent bereavements, my most painful losses, Fresnel and Lucien loom up and seep into the expectant silence. It would take all day to make those who loved me realize that in every man's life there is an infinity of nights, that in these nights there are drugged nights which don't wake up with the sun, and in every crazy night, tombs burst open and yield up models of the dead which are anchored in the infinity of unsubdued grief.

With taboos going off in my head like Catherine wheels, I stop for a break on the edge of town. The cemetery has been tamed by fresh lime, the artificial season of oleander and the overpowering smells of *tafia* and *piment-bouc*. Led by a stream of nymphs-for-a-day, the dance conquers this place of reverence, stands in the way of regrets bewildered by the swagger of the festival. Everything seems to justify its being in leaf. On a pathway lined by tombs, their tops decked out in finery, I sit down to cut grooves in a stolen candle. My keen affection struggles in the furrows that my nails dig in the wax. My body regains its liking for frenzy. Sighs come out of my sorrow. The dead know how to love at the opening of the festival, the beginning of reverence.

The wind has stocked up with ragged songs, shattered footsteps which drown out the last of the sobbing that usually precedes the procession. My prayers, incredulous at so much hysteria, become physical under the insistent caresses I keep warding off. It is a daydream that has real power over my search. I am convalescing from love.

It needed this woman to bring me back to the performance. The way she arrived laughs in the face of all moderation. None of my senses dare try to explain her unexpected presence. The cemetery is a place of confusion strewn with unquiet dead, with lost ghosts. People talk of freed zombies who are waiting for the moment to come out of their daze. They are everywhere. They scorn the terrible fear of death. The woman is in a trance. In her frantic dance she displays her sex to me, working away at it with a hot pepper soaked in cane alcohol. Because I am constantly rubbing against the reality of this ritual, I know she is not bluffing.

Stifling smells. Dances of whirling waists. Songs without rhythm. Everyday words on every wavelength. Her voice rises and tunes in the mood to the right frequency.

"Fresh blood will replace dry blood. We haven't seen anything yet in this country. I see days coming when hands will take up machetes for the great bale-wouze*. Aagh! Port-au-Prince, my girl, the rape will be first class.*

In the future at the gates of the city, Cité Soleil will meet Pétion-Ville for a fight that will be like the passing of the last tank. Woe to them who don't lay down their weapons and their medals at the feet of the departed. The town will be stormed by the seven secret societies of Léogâne and Arcahaie. The dead will console the dead. The dance of the guédés *will be everywhere, every day, until the end of time.*

Leave this town by the first plane, the first boat, the first dream. When the mutilated dead march on the capital under orders of the great general, Baron Samedi, none will be spared and none will fail at the next passing. The land is no longer what it was. It is no match for so many people cut down while they were asleep, for the dead nailed down in their coffins regretting that they haven't lived. All the living are guilty. Responsible."

With the silence she returns to normal. The dance dies away. The pain flares up. Like a child waking after a restless night, she is amazed to see my eyes still fixed on her lips. She turns her head away, gathers up her once-white skirt and tries to move her legs, numbed by her swollen, burning sex. She turns round. Her eyes are searching for the threatened future. She refuses to believe in what is left of her prophecy.

---

* The great cleansing.

10

A T THE CARREFOUR DE L'AVIATION, a day is torn up. People pack their bags of wounds and disappear along the potholed road that is oblivious to the call of the stars. The column winds, solitary in its night march.

The Delmas road is covered with large patches of dried mud, a sign of the last flood. If this country was the same, all we would have to do is spray life with water bowsers every December. On the first of January we would celebrate the baptism of a brand new country without any manufacturing faults. The long line of people is still silent. Now and then it lets out a deep sigh, a question mark over an uncertain tomorrow. For some time the nights have been so long that people are afraid that, one dawn, they won't be able to break the ice to let out the cockcrow. Everyone is going home. Which home? It is the daily rendezvous, the gathering for the little scene at the end of the day. One crowd, two thousand, ten thousand Haitians, one sigh, different songs, God of all the flavours, president for life until the next coup d'état, millions of dried-up hopes waiting for a night without faith or law.

I know these people who are walking. I am witness to their journey. I can predict the route they will take. The people from the markets of En-bas-la-Ville have to stop at the far side of the Carrefour Péan before scattering to the four winds. Aéroport, Cité Cadet, Cité Militaire, Aviation, Saint-Martin,

Solino, district by district, the news on the street will become a chameleon.

It is time to be getting home. Despite the fear of Lucien's dried blood which comes back to me, violent, threatening, I head for Pétion-Ville with a half-hearted plan to skirt round the city. I have learnt to avoid the main entry points, to change my route depending on the day or the prevailing mood. And it is now after eight at night and the town is getting dangerously empty. In a few hours, the masters of midnight, the squadrons of death, will fill the streets in search of the heart of the silence. At every crossroads, cigarette and hot rum sellers set out their packets and bottles. They are privileged people, allowed to confront the night. The lucky man at Lector Market even has a big truck battery to power his Japanese stereo and a light bulb. Everyone has their turn. Everyone has their use. It is in the nature of things that there are salesmen who serve the mysterious workings of the night.

The hot rum seller sets up, the weather changes its clothes. Doors close on plans for nightmares. The lights go out one by one. And because we don't laugh any more in this country after a certain time of night, all you can hear is the crying of a child who hasn't had enough to eat, the retching of someone spewing up their gastro-enteritis. How many bogeymen will be cursed by helpless mothers tonight? Finally I decide to go home. Since I have no reason to hide, I will go to the back room of my shop and wait for Fresnel who won't come, not tomorrow or after that. I get no pleasure from hiding. The night knows its hunting ground. Here, elsewhere, all the walls have ears.

It was with my Jew's instinct that I came back to this town, which is darker than anywhere else. For me, abandoning your business is like getting out of your tomb. I have a shopkeeper's destiny to fulfil. If I had been a historian I would have hidden myself away in a library to understand the past so I could stick a label on the present. I am the inheritor and owner of a shop. I earn my living from the day, even if it is wounded. It is my duty to use my nights of fear to prepare the days. No one can stop me stock-taking, placing orders, selling things to feed those who can bear deep frozen, imported surplus from overfed America. I take on my *de facto* role again, with plans to make the town bow down to a tall hoarding in coloured neon. The name of Assaël will be visible from every direction, sending the message to the palace itself that the Jews have put down roots. I was born into a line of lice that you can't get rid of using ordinary tweezers.

With his mania for other people's history, Fresnel would have been able to give me a historical explanation for why I refuse to admit defeat. The bastard sons of those who colonised Haiti gave themselves the right to decide who lives and does business in this country. When the first Levantines arrived in Haiti, fleeing poverty elsewhere, the country's lords and masters couldn't even tell the difference between a Syrian, a Palestinian and a Jew. We were all the same: vermin who laid out their trinkets in the street, next door to businesses owned by White Europeans who were accepted and integrated. We hid our religion, our age-old quarrels with the Muslims. This compromise allowed us to ruin the European dandies, who were never able to sell anything except their names, to which they had added titles especially for the New World. The Europeans made themselves aristocrats; we made ourselves rich. It is true we have not made much profit from the beaches in this country. But one day we will set up there. Behind a counter, of course.

The shop has not moved. Misfortune is the only thing to leave its mark. I remember that a few days ago, death passed by and mowed down Lucien. How many smothered sighs did he leave in my bed? His memory comes back to me in a burst of silence. From the bedroom comes his collection of messages, adrift among my souvenirs of warmth. I loved his body, tormented by a head that had no feasible plans. Here I am, back in one of my many cells full of memories of happy dawns. Senses numb, I will try and open another window onto the subconscious dance of passions torn apart by morality's unheeded voice.

In my panic to get away I never thought to switch off the radio and its news. It is nine o'clock. It is time to count the spent shells, to measure the depth of the machete blows. I sit in a chair. I light my pipe. I take the news as it comes.

"From a combination of sources. The executive of the governing party has come out in silent protest against the President's militia who, in their alleged ignorance, are turning the country into a no-life zone. This morning a people's deputy, a member of the party executive and a personal friend of the President, was attacked by young militants from Bel-Air. It appears the people no longer acknowledge their leaders. The people accuse them of blinding the President with their new wealth. For their part, the militia denounce, among other things, the way their status as guardians of the Revolution has been trivialised.

If this news is confirmed, in the next few days we will almost certainly see a ministerial reshuffle, a suspension of parliament, government by direct rule and, who knows, an official recognition of the militia's effectiveness as the only ones capable of suppressing the nights of rebellion in this country."

PART TWO

1

HAITI IS THE LAND of the seven ways, the seven crosses, of all the truths. To get to the bottom of a problem you have to knock on more than one door. That is what the old people say. And they have lived. If no one else, they at least can claim to know this country. In Haiti, everything is abnormal.

One of my customers woke up one morning to find her leg swollen like the trunk of a *mapou* tree. I told her to go and see the Cuban doctors, who are renowned as masters of the art of healing. After numerous examinations the doctors told her the leg could not be saved. Flouting this diagnosis, her family came and took her out of hospital. Two weeks later the woman looked fit enough to run a marathon. She had taken the alternative way. That's Haiti for you. You have to see all the cards before throwing in your hand.

I decided to take my troubles to the court of the invisibles. Lucien is dead. I know that for certain. A bullet doesn't forgive. But it's different with Fresnel. His case is still open. He might be in prison, he might be dead. If it turns out to be the latter, I won't be able to rest until I know how it happened. And anyway, no secret is safe in Port-au-Prince. You just have to know how to go about things. If I have to winkle out the truth with tweezers then I will, however forbidden it might be.

Three stations, three chances. To start with I intend to go and see the Missionary on the Mountain. His influence extends over the whole country. He has contacts everywhere. The preachers of Pastor Johnny Bell take the Good News to the remotest corners of the land. There is no doubt that these same preachers act as informers for the central office of the Mission. In my opinion, Pastor Johnny Bell is the leader who has by far the only reliable and effective network in the country. "Everything works for the good of those who love God." The Missionary loves God and knows the things and the people of this country.

If the pastor has trouble ridding me of the slings and arrows of my grief, I won't think of giving up. I will knock on other doors. On Zaccharias's, of course, the head of the army of the wild nights. If my journey takes me into the passages of the underground, mystic world, I will follow in the footsteps of my guide, Edner the *hougan*.

2

Y OU WOULD HAVE TO BE an American missionary to get your gardener to make two ordinary hedges stand up at right angles with the mean-minded intention of protecting a path. The Bells' house is furtive. Even in Haiti, this family can't get away from the image of the little house on the prairie. It is a sign of divine blessing. Milk and honey flows in the pond of promised fish. Who would imagine that a huge, filthy, sleepwalking town has set off towards the Mountain intending to conquer it? Port-au-Prince is striding in other directions. As a town spreads itself out, each new strip of land gained becomes its own, bears its imprint in years to come. I have seen nothing. I know nothing. Porte-au-Prince is climbing. The headquarters of the American Baptist Mission had better keep its distance.

Protestants, as embodied by this family, live for the struggle, the fight against evil. Port-au-Prince is Sodom. Port-au-Prince is Gomorrah. The Protestants of Haiti are already half-way to Heaven. The rest of their road has to be sown with conversions, with those who have returned to the fold for lost sheep. A true Haitian Protestant does not mix with the world. By 'world', they mean a way of life that is far from the presence of God. No trips to the cinema. No alcohol, no cigarettes. Dances, public festivities are forbidden. Politics is not allowed. A Protestant is just a passive citizen, no more no less, who claims his place in Heaven. You must give to God what is God's and to Caesar what is Caesar's.

There is heaven on earth. A white child falls off his pony. His mother, wearing a flowery skirt, lets out a devout "My God". The child gets up, wiping a dewdrop from his jumper. The mother takes him in her arms and all the Haitians in the vicinity begin to pray. Even when he is the child of a missionary, a little American always remains what he is: reinforcements from the centre of the world, a rope hanging down from America to take the star-spangled banner everywhere. Fresnel told me that the chairman of the Mission had all the native children with access to the residence and the Sunday school vaccinated, before letting any missionary's children go there.

Single-handed, I am every part of a lumbering procession pushing the wreckage of its life that is abandoned to silence. There are so many gates that will open at the sound of my whining voice, which barely hides the wounds inflicted by a sun that has gone sour. Or into someone's back pocket? I search for a day in the impenetrable past. In the name of criminal excesses, of cries smothered by the fog, I mean to find the source that makes the big secrets of this country grow.

Seventeen times my tongue silently rehearses its speech. It will break its silence to ask for help, to find Fresnel or perhaps his body. My tongue has known days of rapture with Fresnel's body. It can still taste the quivering saltiness, the touch of a skin that shatters into a thousand dreams. I have already encountered the presence of the Bells. They come to stock up with American goods on the rare occasions they come down from the mountain to confront the heat, the misery and the chaos of Port-au-Prince. Even if you wrote it in blood, they would refuse to understand that a man can love a man. Lousy American hypocrites! Everyone knows the puritan's song: God does not wish … the Holy Bible forbids … but this doesn't stop them moving in political circles without actually getting involved in politics.

From time to time government ministers come to taste Mrs Missionary's famous doughnuts. More than one claims to have seen the venerable pastor get a professional and/or social visit from the President. It goes without saying that people regard the clique of missionaries as CIA agents, anti-communist Neanderthals, post-colonists. They get involved everywhere, supporting the people of Haiti in their enormous need for spiritual and material food. The Mission runs more than three hundred schools, fifty health centres, two hospitals; not counting the road-building projects, professional training, re-forestation, and support for agriculture and crafts.

The blessed court of the Mission is a catalogue of unusual images. It is the central office of a vast network of churches and associated activities. Everything is run from this court. The Mission rarely uses contract workers. It has its own engineers, doctors, theologians, teachers, its own agronomists, its own fleet of vehicles. The offices of the different departments all revolve round the church, whose cross can be seen for miles around. Like worker ants, the pack of labourers, owned by God and managed by the Mission, bustles about in the warehouse which is piled with humanitarian aid in the form of food, medicine and building materials.

Creole is the order of the day here. The Americans never speak English to the Haitians. Between themselves they understand each other. It took ages before I realised that all the Haitians who work for the Mission speak Creole with the same accent as the Americans. The pastor is white. The White man is good. His word comes from God. So does his accent.

Naturally, there is also a mad woman. She is part of the furniture. She is obsessed, she has the God disease. She has gentle eyes and a new and holy Bible. She talks about God to everyone. She hands out the Good News for free, without any aggression. Just for the pleasure. Just out of madness.

"Blessed is he who accepts Christ and makes Him his driver. Man is nothing but a truck, and the only experienced driver is Jesus, the only Son of God. Trust Him with your life and He will wipe the mark of the Devil and the wicked from your brow. Be welcome in the House of God and accept the Light. If you remain deaf to my call, you will have missed one of the last chances to be among the chosen elect. You might well be rich, young and healthy. None of that can protect you. Haiti is going to collapse. Nothing can stop the plan of destruction which the devil has set in motion through politicians who are murdering the institutions, nights that steal memories, children with wounded days. Convert, or leave this cursed land."

The mad woman's hand takes hold of her skirt. Her eyes follow an imaginary flight of migrating birds. And, having spread the Word, her voice fades away. I continue along my road towards the Light. The pastor's house exudes grace.

3

FOR MORE THAN FIVE MINUTES I have been in an enormous living room with an open view. Given my anxiety, life closes up over this space. No one has ever sinned in this room. It exudes saintliness. Above the door are the words: *God is the invisible host in this house*. The décor is in good taste, very *Haitian Lifestyle*. Even the yellow imitation leather sofa, so dear to Americans, has not found a place here. The transistor drags me back to reality. It is the only thing that everyone has in common in this country: the news.

> *"Our correspondent in the north of the country has just told us about an event which, in the opinion of experts on political turmoil, will be a terrible blow to the current regime. Following an altercation between two representatives of the government in the north, the life Deputy of the town of Cap-Haïtien, the first antagonist, gunned down the mayor of the town with seventeen bullets. We consider it necessary to remind you that both men are members of the same political party, that of the President, the government, the absolute majority in Parliament, all the director generals, and of the starving people, etc."*

With perfect timing, the pastor comes in the door and turns off the radio. The news obviously gets on his nerves. I understand. I am sick of it too; except that my curiosity is a motivation without logic. I try and understand the dawning of days in half-tint, the disappearance of my loved ones.

"I'm sorry to have kept you waiting. I wasn't sure I wanted to visit with you" he says. "I know you are a homosexual. But since God is love and forgiveness, I must just make it clear that I have agreed to see you as a director of conscience and not as a friend. God loves you and wants to cleanse you of your sins."

I knew I was going to be up against a morality specialist. But I never imagined he was sufficiently interested in me as a person to be aware of my sexual orientation. I have always been discreet about my private life. What had I done to deserve the coup de grâce before the conversation even started? Still, he might be God's representative on earth, but I am a Jewish shopkeeper: a good reason to negotiate.

"Pastor, I'm sorry to keep you from your work, which is so important for the spiritual and material well-being of this people who are spurned and in need of shepherds. But I know that God's house is open to all his sons, regardless of their race or sexual orientation. And I would feel more comfortable if you treat me as a person who is homosexual rather than saying I am a homosexual."

"I hope the purpose of your visit is not to give me the reasoned, academic argument for accepting differences. I am not a racist, despite my strong conviction that Haitians are incapable of logical analysis. I assume you are not intending to ask me to tolerate a practice that is defiling and against nature, if I may refer to the holy dictates of the Bible."

To keep the discussion on the right track, I steer away from home truths. The pastor is not above suspicion. I know his activities do not stop at preaching the Word. To be able to reconcile religious fervour with wealth, you have to have good outward defences. And in any case I need to ask him a favour. I know he can help me, despite my being a sinner. I am looking for Fresnel, that is all.

I explain what my problem is, making a point of looking him in the eye. He understands. I know from experience that there is a solidarity of colour in Haiti. He and I are both foreigners and white. We are united by a kind of primal need: the need to conspire against this people. We are both in business. We both do well out of it. He senses that I envy him. He knows I do. I too would like to traffic in the lives of my congregation, to be permanently exempt from customs duty, be a guest of the President, get paid for lobbying.

Even though he is reported missing, Fresnel would understand why I persist in steering a situation in a direction where, *de facto*, I might get caught out.

I was afraid of having to keep quiet, and thus lying indirectly so as to be able to keep him a little longer; to prolong the pleasure of feeling that I am waiting for him, for some play of his body or his eyes.

My attempt at a public declaration of love. It is a justifiable way of calling a halt to my most intimate torments. I know reality when I hold it in my hand. Even in the joy of feeling his response of bold, clear desires lived and shared, I keep on making a break with steps I mustn't take, with unknown dances I must avoid.

It is a time of my life for intense absence, forcing me to accept, or (worse) make do with conservative, reactionary solutions. I search the expanse of mirror which is his life, his journeys and his roots. As delirium takes hold of me I want to stay in the tracks, in the depths of his desires.

Fresnel once promised to tell me about his outlawed dreams, his crimes of intent. I am still waiting. I have known days when I planned departures that were definitely provisional or provisionally definite. But sadly I am just a lover in love.

4

Once during my life

WHO DOESN'T KNOW Zaccharias? I met this man only once, by chance in my comings and goings from the customs. But I have never forgotten him. Everyone has always known him. His power is stamped into the memory of this country. At the customs he shook my hand and slipped his card into my pocket. He was in his private fiefdom: the public service. This gentleman is nothing. No official function whatever. Yet this country has always belonged to him for having supported the underground foundations of the regime in power. Our first contact was no more than a glance. He looked me straight in the eye. I did the same. I knew his name, the gallons of blood, emotions and pain that went with it.

He introduced himself with the smile of the eternal victor. He wanted to know what I was trying to see in his eyes. Being a shopkeeper, I have to know the games that all the raging rivers play. Great oak trees can be swept away, while a few wood shavings easily survive. The main thing is to know how to react. I have mastered the art of selling trinkets. To earn the right to bear my name I perform a thousand acts of persuasion every day. When I told him that the President, his President and that of all Haitians black and white, rich and poor, had said, "if you are afraid of someone you must look them in the eye", he relaxed. The beast drew in its claws to see so much political skill in a White, obviously a foreigner.

Next to his power there no doubt lives a man who sometimes notices that he is keeping company with terrible evil. Only pain can understand pain. To hear people talk about Zaccharias you could easily believe that he rules everyone, even the President. Even his faults and insensitivity have not made a crack in his shell as underground head of government for life. Yet everyone tells the story of the day he had all the schools in the Republic closed, to give a little boy time to learn his lessons and do his homework. This took a day. He met this little boy, a real son of the people, in tears one Monday morning. He found out what was upsetting him and took the necessary decision. It was a fait accompli, odd and barbaric. No one dared say a word, not even the Minister of Education.

The whole country lives with him. No one knows him. Who can say why Zaccharias lives his life in the silence of others? He is like a shadow that you can't drive away when it lays itself at your feet at midday. Anything that is said about him always shatters on a wall of fear and anxiety. Nonetheless, he does business. He helps people get promotion, an appointment. His will is a lifetime guarantee for anyone who has lodged an official petition.

The shop is the echo of the town. The town of the shop is the heart of the country. Behind the counter, my head in my account books, I can't remember all the times I have heard people talk about him, always in a whisper. He has no friends. He provides services for the country's rich and respectable families in return for a night with one of their sons. He likes them young and healthy.

So what can I offer him except my abused childhood, my adult's pain in search of at least one of its loves? His own childhood is a mystery. His history is just a few unremarkable lines that you could find on any poster in the street. He arrived in Port-au-Prince one ordinary morning at the head of a big secret. He walked into the office of a presidential candidate. He came out again the day the candidate became Head of State, proudly sporting the presidential sash, greeted the crowds on the steps of the cathedral. Since then, Zaccharias has haunted the streets of the town in an incurable silence.

I rang him. He agreed to see me. He told me he always remembered the few rare people who dared look him in the eye. I am one of them. I get out an old press cutting from about ten years ago. It has his whole life story in twelve lines, tucked away in a corner of one of the big daily newspapers at election time. Whoever says election says hope and passion.

"From a combination of sources. For a whole week the residents of Haut-Turgeau have been unable to get a wink of sleep. Their nights are being disturbed by the constant pounding of drums and the raucous cries of a certain Zaccharias, as he is known. The distinguished guest of a candidate whom the paper refrains from naming, but whom everyone would definitely recognise, he spends his nights calling on all the gods of Africa, turning the lives of the candidate's unfortunate neighbours into what might be called an election nightmare. According to more than one of them, every evening Zaccharias turns into a strange beast and talks to a crowd of ghosts. He explains to them how to go about voting on the day of the election.

Contacted by telephone, the candidate admits he has been putting up a son of the people who is plagued by violent bouts of insomnia, and who he took in off the street. He feels it is a sign of petty, underhand jealousy on the part of his opponents. The fact that they wish to exploit his altruism, his reaction to the suffering of others for political ends, is behaviour far removed from the urgency of lending a helping hand to those most in need, to the people who liberated this country and who have been robbed by a minority of cheap con men.

The candidate believes that the spirit of democracy, so dear to the other election candidates, gives him the right to invite whoever he wishes into his house without having to give an account of his actions. He is

*a candidate and a citizen. Even at the palace, he will still have the
same rights as any other citizen."*

*"In an upcoming edition of our newspaper, your newspaper of refer-
ence, we will be bringing you the results of our ongoing investigation."*

The investigators took with them, along with the newspaper,
Zaccharias's first moves in the capital. No one heard any
more about it. By a combination of unfortunate circumstances, the newspaper did not survive beyond the first month
of the new regime. The journalists, less dangerous, are perhaps crossing off the days on a huge calendar on the wall of
their cells with a piece of charcoal. The others have joined
the legion of zombies who haunt all the games between the
national palace and the great cemetery of Port-au-Prince.

5

MY FOOTSTEPS CLING TO THE BREATHING of my guide. In the tropics, nightfall always comes as a surprise. Daylight turns deep black without a qualm, without a go-between. I think the day does its best to avoid understanding what goes on on Zaccharias's property. So many words have stopped at the edge of this darkness. I no longer have eyes. All I have left is the stumps of my senses. I am frightened of what I am doing.

The persistence of the night combines with malicious rumours to turn the residence of Monsieur Zaccharias into the set of a horror film. In different circumstances I might have enjoyed the mysterious calm of this place; especially when I think how close it is to the uproar of Port-au-Prince. By isolating this moment I am swept along, already lost in the dénouement of my plans. But a Jew is used to crossings, and not just the short ones. Every day, the number of kilometres travelled by my race in search of a land of transit is as far as the distance from the earth to the moon. Yet this is not our destiny; it is our act of overturning history. The State of Israel is not enough for us.

My guide has a fascinating way of working. He leads the way without worrying about my motives. In a sense he is simply delivering me to his master. Since I was due at six he waited for me, checked my identity, and that was all. Perfectly impersonal, he just made a sign for me to follow him. My naturally bad habits prompted me to keep close on his heels. Direction: second station for Fresnel.

I am always the one who follows, who comes afterwards; we arrive at a colonial-style house with a big veranda like the one in my dreams. Zaccharias, wearing a colourful scarf round his head, holds out an almost friendly hand. With an impeccable gesture he motions me to sit down and turns up the volume of a radio that is in arms reach.

For once I have the terrible impression that the radio really does connect people. Between the breaking up of the silence and the voice of the presenter dissecting the week's events there was my body, which felt the need to direct my slightest gesture towards Fresnel. Unfortunately my desire to yell out my problem fell on deaf ears. The master of the house was listening to the radio. For isn't this country destined to wait for ever for the day that will arrive on the airwaves?

"There has been no news from the meeting that took place this morning between the Minister for Commerce and representatives of shopkeepers in the capital. It must be remembered that in his latest public statement, the President accused shopkeepers in the capital of vastly inflating the price of essential goods. For their part, the shopkeepers claim they are victims of a racket run by those in charge of the Customs Service. According to them it is an absolute mafia. The shopkeepers are also complaining about the countless political, social and religious organisations that are exempt from paying customs duty on imported goods that they then sell on at totally uncompetitive prices.

News is just coming in from our city-centre correspondents that at this moment a number of shops are being looted. Out of discretion and a desire for objective reporting, we cannot confirm the accounts of several eyewitnesses, who claim this looting is taking place under the protection of militants who are close to the government and the police."

I am beginning to understand what is so important about my search. By delving into my memory I again see so many dawns, dreamt on the summit of the mountain where our bodies live. The unmoving, imposing darkness of this house gives birth to a time and place to reflect on the past. I have never doubted that at some point in my life I would need to come and see the grand master of the night. I had hidden the card he slipped into my pocket at the customs among samples of useless products that door-to-door sales-man give me.

The card found its way into the place I usually reserve for requests for loans, instalment payments from women who owe the shop money, sponsorship proposals for a football team, a candidate or a group of musicians. My little cache of repul-sive objects has a long memory. Once a month I get it all out and add up my prejudices. Not once have I taken the time to imagine this scenario. Assaël in the position of applicant, up against Zaccharias on Zaccharias' territory. I am afraid of power and all who serve it.

I once asked Fresnel why power in Haiti always surrounds itself with mysterious people like Zaccharias. He replied that it is power which is mysterious, and petty crooks hover round it.

I listened to the news. My reserves of clear-thinking were plunged into a whirlwind of words, strung together, tossed about at the whim of my host. I dare to understand my reac-tion. Sitting in front of me is the unofficial midwife of the revolution. To bolster my courage I keep telling myself that I am just somewhere, with a human being who will understand that I haven't come to him as a shopkeeper, but as a simple Jew with a broken heart.

"Goodness! What do they want this time?"

Zaccharias's voice carves open the silence. He turns off the radio and motions to a good-looking man to bring us a drink.

He continues:

"This country is in danger of getting into a state of institutionalised chaos. I don't understand how the government can endorse such behaviour. I've spoken to the President about it. You can't run a country without the backing and the support of the business community. The people are like children. They want everything immediately. On no account must the public's demands be allowed to threaten the safety of those who have the means and the intelligence to create jobs, to keep the economy going. God almighty!"

Zaccharias empties his glass. His gaze stands between us. Shady. Withering.

"And what do you think? What future is there for a country without its brains and its job creators?"

I daren't point out to my colourfully-dressed host that my being here has nothing to do with the world of politics. A shopkeeper by trade, my reply reveals my policy of half-measures.

"I think you're right. But on the other hand, the business sector could be more flexible. The government's demands are justified, in that they tend to keep the cost of living down. The people are hungry. It's the responsibility of those running the country to protect the interests of the people who elected them as a matter of priority. I think it's journalists who prevent the unity of this … "

I settled for a reactionary and treacherous reply. Fear was making my survival instincts work at full speed.

6

I AM DESCENDED FROM THE PEOPLE who invented exile. A long time ago, almost as long as the memory of history, we were the masters of every expression of distance. It is not ironic if every Jew inherits several thousand years of exhausted footsteps, of suitcases done up on the outskirts of every town. A Jew has tough skin. It brings lands with it from everywhere, heavy, different lands. The key to the universe is in the middle of the ark that we are pushing towards our touched-up tomorrows.

I left Zaccharias with the desire to make an emergency stop at the nearest bar. I need air, music, something to get me back on the road. This guy is either mad or wise. And there I was, thinking I would go to his house and not come back. I imagined him living in underground tunnels in the depths of a mountain, with zombies in every nook and cranny. I also thought I would be greeted by a large devil to whom I would hold out a cow's hoof to stop him crushing my hand if he insisted on shaking it. I can't get over my surprise. Not the slightest trace of blood at his house. Just a particular kind of court in the early evening, a master's house, a welcoming host.

There is a country where the parameters are inverted, collide with each other, stand logic on its head. Miracles have no meaning here. I live in this town, capital city of a bizarre country that has dared stay alive despite four centuries of being cursed. No one remembers when it was that the struggle simply to survive began. No one dares predict when the end will come. Zaccharias, however, has a plan. This presumed guardian of blood, collected every night at the crossroads in Port-au-Prince where all the channels meet, has set himself up on the road to the future. This country will end up transforming my sceptic's destiny.

My father taught me the history of our people. It is made up of a collective will for the future with pride of place given to destiny. Travelling people like us have no right to turn our backs on our identity. We know exile. All Jews have been there. It is our common point of reference. Each of our communities brings new facts picked up from brushing against other cultures, other ways of life. My people are an encyclopedia, a collection of passports. The plans for the future I cling to go beyond this country, which gets a mouthful of water whenever it tries to swim. I am from here, I earn my living here, I lose my lives; but my ambitions are much like those of the people of my community.

And by extension, my community is also my loves who have been killed or reported missing. I am firmly convinced that sharing someone's life history is grounds for strong, close ties. Fresnel and I had the same childhood. We always shared the same games. And today we dream of the same everlasting day, the continuity of life. Strange, but the more I move on, the more I get the feeling that Fresnel is not dead. My body has not given me any particular sign. My sense of bereavement dies down. Only the struggle remains.

If I had dared ask Zaccharias to help me in return for 'moral' support for his cause, I would go round the whole country four more times if needs be. I am a Sephardi: history has never come up with an easy life for us. We are everywhere in the world, our will like a tool, searching for the colour of our earliest days. Fresnel is just a stage and we will survive. My mouth opens to cry out my pain.

7

ON THE ROAD OF MY SEARCH, I have travelled through nights, I have listened to music. When the miseries endured by the first Jews to arrive in Haiti suddenly take possession of my bundle of memories, I imagine having a chance to make myself heard. I am from a rich community that has no political allegiances. Gone are the days when Jews were undesirables. My father, who was determined to keep the memories alive, talked to me years ago about the Jews' quarrels with the mulattos. At the time the latter held the political reins. Although like us they were foreigners, they had no desire to share power. What was more, the Jews who came to Haiti did not behave like Europeans. They were in the same category as Levantines, good for making lamb kebabs and eating couscous. To succeed in this country you had to be a foreigner of European birth.

Then the Americans occupied the country. They looked everywhere for collaborators. Our community was forged out of good relations. It was able to leave the parched countryside and gradually set itself up in the capital. The Europe-lovers were pushed out to make more room. And us? We come from nowhere. We have no final destination. We just honour the road. Our journey will be over on the day the world ends.

Fresnel had helped me collect pieces of paper, press cuttings from the end of the last century. He advised me to do this in the days when we were wearing out the seat of our trousers at the Collège Saint-Martial. It was one way among others of understanding the Father Superior who had forbidden me to do anything but go into business. I could have gone to university, like Fresnel. But I simply did not have the right. A Jew keeps to his place. It is part of his destiny. From time to time I look at these old papers. They make me sad. They encourage me. It all depends on the tension, the sounds that reach me.

Zaccharias talked to me about this bitter period of our history and I had been thinking that he knew nothing at all. He told me the Blacks and the Jews ought to join forces to reverse the course of history. When I told him I was a foreigner, he explained it was the same for Blacks. This is a stolen land; those in power have to play hopscotch. My relationship with Fresnel made an impression on him: Black and White. It is a sacred union. He admitted he was also homosexual. Simply out of passion.

I take an official text from my pocket, copied onto a page from an exercise book. I have kept it on me for years. It is like a door that opens onto courage, a passport to the struggle.

Extract from The Official Gazette of the Republic of Haiti *on the eighth day of the first month of Year Eighty of Independence.*

By decree of the President of the Republic following a recommendation from the Council of Ministers, ratified by Parliament and with the aim of ensuring social peace, the following has been decided:

1. *Foreign nationals belonging to the Jewish Muslim community are banned from Haitian territory with effect from the publication of this decree in* The Official Gazette of the Republic of Haiti.
2. *Property and real estate belonging to those affected by this measure will be sold to the highest bidder and the sums collected will be paid to the former owners, after the deduction of taxes and any other costs, should these be due.*

> *This decree, although contrary to our tradition of hospitality, is motivated by the constant complaints from our Christian fellow citizens who have duties when faced with the heresy spread by the Jewish Muslims. Indeed, the latter, not content with ridiculing consumers by selling cheap rubbish, use every means of persuasion to turn the population away from the teaching of the Bible and the Catholic faith. Our duty is to protect the people from barbaric and unorthodox practices such as the circumcision of boys, the ritual slaughter of animals and fasting on Saturday, among others. Our country, which is constantly in search of the Light and the principles of an enlightened country, cannot permit such dubious activities. It is our duty as a government to lead our citizens along the path to progress.*

Confronted with so much injustice and prejudice, the Jewish community resorted to every conceivable tactic. There were more than five thousand of them from North Africa, Turkey, Spain, Italy and Portugal. Long cohabitation with Muslims had transformed their original Judaism. But they came to Haiti in search of a land. They had never behaved like colonists. From the moment they arrived they worked hard for the shopkeepers here, slept twelve to a room. They more than paid their way in this country. As usual, they pulled through. And at the time this decree was published, the wealth of the Jews accounted for at least a tenth of the wealth of the country.

Several families went back into exile. Out of habit, out of having to. Now, I think they were right. A lot of families, including mine, stayed on and converted to Catholicism. They helped build churches. They financed a revolution. And the decree was revoked. Then, the whole community understood that a Jew was henceforth a Haitian who runs his shop and pays the political class.

I am a descendant of those who chose to stay. Inside me I carry the legacy of history, and I live with my own: my love.

And I think I behave decently towards other people. Being in business has never driven me to make a quick profit or become famous. I serve the poor, the rich, the White, the Black, the victim and his executioner. I have always been understanding with customers who are broke, with those who are uncouth. My shop lives by other people's sorrows. I have done my best to help the hungry who pass by my door. What power could the forces of evil have over me?

8

THE RIVER HAS GONE MAD. It is not sleeping in its own bed. In the living memory of Artibonitians, no one has ever seen it in this state. For three days its roaring has made the Cahos mountains shake. Only the gods and Port-au-Prince could do something. The farmers of Artibonite sowed rice; what they will reap is the American wheat given to disaster victims.

Perhaps I chose the wrong door to enter the Artibonite valley, to launch myself towards another station on my route. The river passed through last night. It got here before me. It is six hours since this cross-country vehicle spewed its bile over the trail. It is moving on, but slowly. On both sides of the road the farmers are draining the water that is left. It is a distressing sight. To each his sins. To each his misfortunes.

The river is sure to come back tonight, crying like a wounded giant, to dump the cultivated soil it picked up in the hills in people's bedrooms. The farmers are used to life being an upward climb. It is the only way they have of seeing what lies ahead. When the river is not driving them out, it is the head of section's whistle. If it is not the whistle, it is the landowners' bullets.

Artibonite, a valley full of holes, darkness and graveyards, is a land of water and mudslides. Here, distances are still measured in ells, as in the past. The future of this place is Port-au-Prince's business. Lucien was born in this valley. The land his parents worked had been in the family for more than three generations. At an early age, Lucien learnt to get down on his knees and make the millet and sweet potatoes grow. Admittedly it was a hard life, but the family always had enough to live on. Their troubles started when the Germans, at the request of the old regime, built a dam on the river. With the water finally under control, the land became fertile. The rice began to grow. To show their gratitude the farmers went to the capital. They celebrated for three days. Danced outside the palace, wished the President to hold office for life. The President received them in the palace. With his ministers he ate their rice and agreed to be President for life.

Port-au-Prince set up cooperatives to help the farmers. Port-au-Prince put technical missions in place to pass on specialist knowledge. Port-au-Prince sent soldiers to make the valley secure. Port-au-Prince sold the land and its farmers, the farmers and their land, for the good of the nation. An American company was given the concession to export the naturally-grown rice to the dinner tables of rich people far away, and to import surplus foodstuff from the United States.

The farmers took refuge in Port-au-Prince, on the workers' housing estate. The ones who stayed behind took leasehold contracts, payable in shares of the harvest. Three parts for the owner, one for the farmer. When the harvest is not good they are thrown off. If they put up a fight they are accused of being communists and hunted down like rabbits. The valley is at war with Port-au-Prince. Only the river can make its voice heard and banish the bad air.

I lower the car window a fraction. The sounds carry the song of struggle: wheels spinning in the mud, farmers' buckets scraping on the stones, an uprooted tree that tries to cling on to the bank. I have the feeling that I am in the middle of a scene from the end of the world. I am truly alone in pursuing a life that I meet at all the dangerous crossroads along the great road. Life is getting ahead of me, dribbling with my desires, taking crazy shortcuts.

I have a meeting with Edner, the head of more than half the secret societies in the country. It seems he is even more feared than Zaccharias. They tell me he makes the dead speak from two centuries ago. He has his own cave in the back of beyond, which he uses for difficult cases or reasons of state security. I hope I will get the solution from him. If not, where do I go next?

9

NOT EVEN A SHUDDER OF FEAR since I got though the second station. This is the next one, and I don't know how much further I have to go. My road must end eventually—I sense it is pointing to the way out. I live too much in the hope of a flowering not to believe it. I reconcile myself with logic and drink my water calmly. For a quarter of an hour I have been sitting across the street from Edner's courtyard. Scattered drumbeats shatter the peace of the district. People come out, others go in. It is past ten o'clock at night. The road is long; my ardour turns to ice at the scene I am imagining.

A car pulls up level with mine. A large four-wheel-drive Mercedes. The driver winks at me. Everyone understands each other. It is the German Consul General. Someone else chasing after froth or hope. This country is just like a village. We are all searching for the same opening. Each of us gives whatever name we want to our basket of sorrows gathered up after every night of madness. One person has a need to understand. Another leaps into the waves to save who he can. No one comes from here. We are all foreigners who have been bitten by this country. When the virus takes hold you daren't leave. Haiti has the knack of embedding itself deep down in the souls of those who come here.

"Tout moun dòmi
lakay
mwen sèl ki nan seren
Tout moun dòmi
lakay
mwen sèl ki nan seren
zanmi zanmi kole kole
*s am jwenn se li ma pran"**

The wait—for I don't know what—becomes delirious, dizzying. This song marks the beginning of the blind festival. The night will tremble. All it can do is keep its hours in time with the rhythm of the drums and the tuppenny tin bugles. I get out of the car, mind churned over by the meanings that my eyes and my nightmares give to this song. It is vital for what I am doing to separate my prejudices from the need that drives me on.

The peristyle round the courtyard is lit up in red and by candles. Solitude brings a lump to my throat at the sight of so much sparkling. My head wants me to walk in there, my body backs away. The festival is too intense to be real. The dance is passionate, it carves out my presence. In order to grow up with this country I grew up with voodoo. But every beat that draws a cry of protest from a drum has always reminded me that I, too, come from somewhere far away, far away from here.

A man comes and stands in front of me. He takes my hand and drags me with him into the middle of the dancers. He is in a trance; his eyes speak the language of a ravaged land. His touch is reassuring and impartial. He has a real farmer's hand, rough and broad. He drags me into his dance, through the *vèvès*

---

* "Everyone is sleeping/barricaded in the house/I am alone with the night/everyone is sleeping/barricaded in the house/I am alone with the night/my friends and I form a circle/I set off on the hunt/I won't let anything get away."

and the candles, and leads me into a room beyond the dance floor and its ceremony, to Edner the *hougan*. Edner motions me to sit down and hands me a half-empty bottle of rum.

"Have a grown-up drink, brother" he says. "You need it to forget all the miles."

"Thanks for giving me a good welcome. I'll do my best to be worthy of the honour."

He looks at me, sways his head from side to side and points out his friends all round him. One of them is the Consul who winked at me a quarter of an hour ago.

"The gods of Africa are from every race. In my house, as long as I still have the privilege of serving the *lwa*, everyone is treated as an equal. Here we all drink straight from the same bottle. All wealth is dust. It only takes a gust of wind and it is scattered to the four corners of the earth. Here"—he gives me a garish red tunic—"you are worthy of these clothes. We will talk about your problem tomorrow. Tonight is a celebration. Even when the river decides to make our poverty worse, we have to show the gods that we really do want to see another day. If they see we are hanging on to life, they will calm the river."

A woman of about sixty holds out her hand as if to ask me to dance. I look at Edner. He approves. With the first pirouette she takes away all my awkwardness. Her crumpled body has no trouble following the raging rhythm of the drums. I look into her eyes—I shouldn't have. Her gaze is fixed. She is not even moving her eyes. She is just a trembling body which holds on to me, hard but gently.

Sweat, alcohol and the drum that works on my senses get the better of me. She sits on a chair and lays me on her legs as if in a dream. She takes out a handkerchief, wipes her face. With a light, almost maternal touch, she wipes my face with her handkerchief. From what little I know, this is a privilege. She wants to pass on a certain art of understanding. Her mouth opens like a doll's and begins to speak:

"Ay pitit mwen, wout la long. Se pa de pas dlo ou pa travèse avan ou rive la epi ou pa konnen kombyen ou rete. Peyi sa s'on maleng envlimen.

M' santi ou blese jis nan kè w'. Lavi jenn gason isi pa fasil. Tande, tout lwa gason se masisi. Yo danse nan tèt moun yo vle. Soti sou lakou a limen yon bouji nwa anba pye mestiyen ki fé kwen baryé a. Se pou mechan fout rann ou sa w ap chèche a."*

None of those watching us show any surprise. I have been aroused by an old woman who is just skin and bone. She burst in on my secrets. Everyone finds this normal. Perhaps the others have not seen or heard a thing. In these circles, mystery is part of daily life. She must have taken me off into a world quickly invented for the two of us. The time for asking questions will come later. I am here because I have no choice. Everything I am offered is welcome.

I leave the room, like I have been told to. The night greets me with a gentle breeze. I light my candle. The flame flickers, dies down. It burns well. I even get the impression that it is controlling the wind. It is so delicate, so tiny in the face of so much frenzy, yet it keeps to its task of melting the wax. It will go out with the feeling of a job well done. I am a flame; I am inventing short cuts and stairways for my road.

---

* "My son, the road is long. I imagine all the fords you crossed to get here. The worst thing is you have no idea what is waiting for you. This country is a wound. A great big wound of hardships with a nasty expression on its face.

"I know your heart is wounded. Life is never easy for the men of this country. But listen to me: the gods of Africa are all hermaphrodites. They mount women and men as the fancy takes them. You will go out and light a black candle under the big tree next to the main gate. The wicked must give you back your confiscated dreams."

10

NEVER DID THE SUN RISE so arrogantly. The few shadows that remain in the valley are pushed back violently behind the mountain. I have not wasted the merest piece of this struggle, carried on under great, harsh beams of light and to the sound of strange moans. In the distance, the singing of the workers means the level of the river is going down. This unashamed attachment to life makes a sharp contrast with the capital, so bereft of air and laughter. Resigned to being a prisoner of my shop, at the heart of a town that is on the point of imploding, I take a deep breath of the fresh, eternal dew of my thoughts.

With her bare feet, an adolescent girl draws an angel on the wet ground. Her movements, although fated to create a fleeting work of art, are like a dance in honour of the earth. In the valley, the earth is still the most beautiful expression of a certain continuity of life. Earth that is washed to its very depths. Earth that is fertile, opening to receive the seed of the rice. Earth that is discreet, complicit, that never rejects the dead or their secrets.

Lost in the colours of a new day, I did not see the procession arrive. Four *hounsis** lead the way for Edner the *hougan*. As they pass by they practically brush against me. The procession moves like an automaton. The sunlight shines through

---

* Girl initiates who assist the voodoo priest during a ritual.

the white robes of the girls and reveals their hips, en route to the place of ritual. The adolescent artist signs her drawing then joins the group at the main entrance to the courtyard. She takes a jug of water from one of the girls. Another of them gives her a bunch of wild basil. One by one she picks off the leaves and rubs them gently. Her gestures are as measured as before. But now her movements are more precise, not as light. She takes her time with her game, makes the leaves give up all their juice. She looks round at the *hougan*, takes two steps back and bows down to place her work at the feet of Edner the *hougan*, who begins his libation.

"Mètrès Klèmezin Klèmèy, oumenm ki gen kle dlo na men w', nou vle de w' mèsi paske ou tande rèl chwal ou yo. Se ou ki ban nou dlo. Men lè nou fè w' fache nou konprann ou anvi fè nou pase tray. Fwa sa a, chay la te lou. Nou mande ou bay pitit ou kouray pou repran travay yo dekwa pou yo jwenn ase mwayen pou ofri w' sa ou renmen. Dlo sa a nou pral jete a tè a se moso kontra pan ou pou respekte té n ap viv kif è nou viv la."*

As soon as the libation is finished, the girls form a circle. Drop by drop, the earth opens up to the holy water. On the ground they mark out a *vèvè*, the sacred space. The *hougan* pours three drops of coffee onto the ground, for the dead, the angels and the saints. Finally he sprinkles the ground with rum and stands gazing at the new day, already captive to its promises.

---

* "Master Agwe, guardian of the destiny of the waters, I hasten to give thanks to you for so mercifully hearing your servants' cries of despair. You have always given us plentiful water. But when you are angry with us, we feel your anger. This time the punishment has been severe.

  We ask you for the courage to work our land. We need the harvest so we can offer you gifts. The water we are going to spill on the ground is our contract by which we promise you to respect the land that gave birth to us."

This is no ordinary working day. The river fell silent on the stroke of midnight. It is time to count up all the working hours that have been lost.

Edner turns to me, hands me a cup of coffee. I pour out the first three drops in a clumsy attempt to copy the gestures of the *hougan*. The strong taste of the earth catches in my throat. As after a storm, life begins to return to normal. Women get out their pots and pans. Children look to see which way the wind is blowing; it will carry their kites up to the clouds that are taking their time to lift. After death there is life. After the libation, the court can live again.

11

I HAVE JUST SPENT THE DAY doing things that seem supernatural to a stranger. It was difficult! Fresnel is not dead. He
is not living deep underground. Edner the *hougan* searched for
him everywhere. Even on the surface of the mass graves. He
did not reply. I don't have detailed knowledge of the mysteries
of this country. But how can you not believe them when you
have always lived in Haiti?

At ten o'clock this morning I was in the arbour playing a
game of dominoes with a group of cheerful, noisy people. I
would have happily spent the day like that if I was on holiday.
But I was here for another reason. I could think of only one
thing: the exact time of my consultation. Interesting as the
game was, I had the feeling of being too close to Fresnel. His
voice came from all sides. I even heard it in the clack of the
dominoes. Absence became a heavy veil, isolating me from
the people nearest me. And I wanted to get back on my road,
to follow the banks of the calmed river. Subdued.

The sun had shaped my memory already. I didn't take
much notice of the scheming sunbeams that shone through
the plaits of the coconut trees. They looked like fragments of
ghosts on the ground. The wind, busy playing hopscotch with
the kites, left its mark on every sway of the coconuts. The
ground shook. Really shook. The kind of shaking that grabs
the pit of your stomach and sets off your survival instincts.

Edner appeared from nowhere and stood in the middle of the arbour. He began to whirl round. Grabbed a bottle of white rum as he passed. In spite of the day, the sun and the wind, he still laid his calloused hands on me, looked at me with his wounded madman's eyes.

The game of dominoes made way for more serious matters. The *hougan* launched into one pirouette after another. It gave me a scare, frankly. With incredible composure, one of his assistants took the bottle away from him and got him under control. He took off Edner's shoes.

"*Ey fout gason! Pile tè a se la fòs ou ye,*"* he boomed.

Edner let him do it. Then the assistant dealt with the *hougan's* trousers, rolling them right up his legs. He tied a red scarf around his right wrist for him, and then disappeared the way he came.

Edner regained his composure, and gestured me to follow him into the room where he worked. A real chaos of colours and strangeness. Here was the silence. Through the translucent haze I could make out four men, crouching in positions of utter collapse. Their neglected bodies were just so many borderless territories inhabited by the gods. The only thing that seemed to defy the silence was a few yellow candles. The *hougan* grabbed one of them and calmly ran his fingernails through the wax. After each turn he stopped and poured a drop of white rum onto the ground in honour of a *lwa* god. His distraction only lasted a moment. At last he sat down in his armchair.

I expected him to get out a pack of cards and ask the usual questions. I had been preparing myself for this game for some time. In cases like this it was supposed to be inevitable. But against all my expectations, he approached the problem differently. Without cards, without rigmarole. He asked me

---

* "Man, you have to tread the land with your bare feet. The land is a source of strength. Tread this land for me."

for Fresnel's photo, his boxer shorts, his hairbrush and seven hundred and thirty-five gourdes and thirty-five centimes. From my scant knowledge of that world, I knew the thirty-five centimes was the share that was due to the gods. The copper coins (seven five-centime pieces) would be blessed and placed in the middle of the first seven crossroads from the peristyle. I hastened to comply. He showed me a mound of earth which to my mind served as an altar, and made my offering.

The four assistants, a queenly soloist and three drummers, backed out of the room. They began to play. The pounding of the drums bounced off the walls and came back, even more deafening, to take possession of the space, of my eardrums, my waiting. Taking advantage of this atmosphere, Edner asked me to come closer and sprinkled me with fresh water from a large earthenware jar. Then he addressed me.

"After this sprinkling of holy water you will become my *pitit-fèy*.* This water comes from a spring upstream. It is pure water. Every Thursday, seven unsullied women fetch water to fill the jar. These women, preferably in the menopause, are the faithful servants of the *lwa* of all the rivers and the sea. You can imagine how angry Agwe, Simbi, Klèmezin Klèmèy would be if this role was performed by women who are menstruating or at a time of great sexual activity. This water will let you pass over into the world of the supernatural, which is the true world of knowledge. You are fortunate to have gods who watch over you."

He baptised me. A minute after I was received as an initiate, he drew a curtain, gave me back the things I had laid out on the mound of earth, and asked me to go into the back room on my own.

Two or three minutes went by. Endless. Edner's voice ripped through the curtain.

"What do you see?"

* Spiritual son.

"Nothing."

"Did someone speak to you?"

"No."

"Are you sure?"

"Yes."

He asked me to come out of the back room. There was a broad smile on his face. He took a mouthful of rum and handed me the bottle.

"I think you've made a wasted journey. It's better that way. I like to see my clients go away happy. Your friend isn't dead. He might be in prison or in exile. Go and confirm it on this side."

"I'd prefer to confirm that he is actually alive. Do you have a way of doing that?"

He did not seem at all bothered by my scepticism. He asked me for a photo of someone close to me who was dead. I got out a photo of Lucien in his Sunday suit. It was a passport photograph that he had had taken for a visa application to the Venezuelan Embassy. He wanted to leave by any means possible. I can't remember how many job applications I had to write for Lucien. He never managed to get a visa to leave the country. Not enough guarantees. After trying the American, Canadian, French and Venezuelan Consulates, his passport was now adorned with more than a dozen refusals.

He asked me to go back behind the curtain, this time with the photo of Lucien. Two minutes later, as if at the height of a storm, the evidence suddenly appeared. Gigantic. Astonishing. Lucien's voice came out of the mist. Staggering.

"Why have you disturbed me? I had to come back to speak to you. What do you want? You saw me die outside your shop and you think the angels of the night will soon be short of bullets. Don't kid yourself. When they haven't got any bullets left they'll get out their machetes. The same ones you ordered from Brazil, Mexico, from everywhere, thinking you were being helpful by selling them.

This country is done for. I feel good on my journey. If you want to talk to me, leave this country. You won't believe me: even dead and six foot under, my killers disturb my abandoned body.

Stop looking for Fresnel in this country. He's in Miami. He wrote to you. But he refuses to send the letter through the post. He knows they will open it. They are everywhere. They won't think twice about killing you to intimidate the other shopkeepers. You are a Jew. Your name is Assaël. You were born with a compass in your hand. You are lucky to have plenty of visas. Leave, and good luck. As for me, I have no regrets, I am setting off on my road again. It is a long one."

As for Fresnel, he will definitely find someone to deliver his letter to you personally. Cursed be the day when we gave power to the voracious leech."

The voice died away, leaving just the sound of interference that had come with it. Without any comment. Edner gave me the bottle again and shattered my inertia.

"Take this bottle. Drink your toddy and leave, go a long way if you have to, in search of your life. You have seen that life goes on indefinitely, beyond death, of course. The important thing is to live to the full all the lives that come along. Leave, my son, and send me a postcard. I am not master of my own destiny. I am here to serve the *lwa*. As long as the sun is allowed to pass over this country, I will have to stay."

12

EVERY YEAR, THE NIGHTS of Port-au-Prince take a lot of lives away on journeys to the other side of the sun. The appeal of the unknown is of no use. Drop by drop you hear the story of hours decimated by resignation. I have just got back to town. Again I use my foreigner's eyes, my foreigner's approach. I have nothing to be ashamed of, considering the dearth of any aid here. The same children are in the same place, sniffing glue. It is their way of drawing on waxed paper. The image they want to create is far removed from the games they are meant to play. The sight of them always takes me back to my own childhood. I feel no remorse; despite this monument to imposed delinquency which adorns itself with yet more decorations each time it makes an appearance. At the root of it is the hand of Brother Pascal, which for so long wandered over my child's body. From one decoration to the next, my past is chequered with unhappy, unsmiling masks. I have spent my life as a target. Yesterday I was a tiny spot to hit. Today I wear glad rags for a land that has died.

Haiti is like a raging river that scours the earth in search of its buried heart. Only by getting angry does it manage to find the treasure chest. When it has finally taken out its heart, it goes back to bed and spends its days watching life moving away on the bank. I know the stories of the heart. I live off Haiti. Passion is a dense fog, and anyone with determination searches for whatever part of childhood they can find. My character is a product of deprivation. How many embraces have I missed since death and fear came knocking at my door?

Despite my long communion with this country, I sense I am missing certain things. Yet they are important for my survival. My attachment to this country is as strong as the fickleness of a thousand ravening vultures. Which of us will return to the same madness a million times? The winner will undoubtedly see the end of the tunnel.

My family has been here for generations. It is normal that I should be marked. I have the feeling of having served. Who hasn't? I have heard Haitians telling anyone who will listen that they will stay like this until the after-season.

I am in the town with the rage of the river still in my ears. I am in the town with Lucien's voice. No. He told me that Fresnel isn't dead. I know he never liked Fresnel, the pretentious little mulatto who hated coming to the shop.

Lucien is free. When he was alive he never spoke to me the way he did in Fresnel's jar. Death is like exile. They both have the power to liberate, from a country, from a social dimension, from preservation.

I take Lucien at his word. For once, the streets of Port-au-Prince don't stick their tongues out at me. My fear is elsewhere. When you have travelled on roads flooded by the river Artibonite, when you return from the depths of mystery, a town, even a ferocious one, is nothing to be afraid of. It has been said that Fresnel's letter will get to me. At this very moment it might be on an American Airlines flight, hidden in the false bottom of a bag. I fly. I glide. The street follows its road. I look after mine. People are talking about the high cost of living. The masters of night are preparing for battle. The President is having his siesta. The radio bellows the latest news.

"The Haitian community in the United States is in turmoil. According to an article published by a daily paper in Miami, the twelve alleged bandits recently lynched by members of popular organisations close to the government in front of pupils from every school in the capital, were members of the opposition party who had planned violent action to weaken the regime. These so-called Zenglendos* *were handed over bound hand and foot to the government by members of their own party. Everyone remembers these tragic events. We did our duty as journalists in exposing the fact that schoolchildren were forced to be present at the execution. Our objectivity required us to present the facts without taking sides. But today we have every right to rebel against this motiveless killing. We believe that no war, even one that is won, is worth a human life. Our people, our fellow countrymen, have sunk to a level of true non-humanity. Our children are living with blood. Our children have only treachery and back-stabbing as examples.*

Once more, and once too often, our national pride has suffered griev-ous harm. We are unable to organise ourselves. Who cannot remember the successful fundraising organised by the opposition in exile? Our reporters on the spot noted that even the Chinese made contributions. The suffering of the people, at the mercy of bad government for almost two centuries, aroused the pity of other countries around the world. The struggle even seemed to catch the attention, too often passive and indirect, of the leaders in the North and of international institutions. But this untimely outrage sadly takes us back to square one.

This will probably be my last news bulletin. The operator has just told me that the Chief of Police telephoned. His men are on their way. They are marching on the radio station, the last bastion of your liberty, your right to information. I knew it had to come. But those who gorge themselves on the pride and the blood of those who have always tried to build cannot escape the revenge of the population of zombies when they come out of their torpor. All the zombies are waiting for is a pinch of salt."

---

* Armed gangsters.

The presenter's voice has just been replaced by the national anthem. Suddenly I want to go home. There is nothing good in store for this town.

For our country
For our forebears
Let us march united

A voice, yet another voice, is going to be crushed against the night. It is true this country really does exist. But it is no longer the majority who think that it will continue to exist without us.

13

WHAT A SHAMBLES, THIS SHOP. It took me three days to find the box of letters from Lucien. For a long time I have kept Fresnel's letters. He writes so beautifully. And now I have got his most recent one. The only one I was prophesised to get. It is in the box with the rest. According to Fresnel's instructions I ought to destroy it. I decided to keep it. It is not as well written as the others. The prose is poor and direct. It's mad, exile. Fresnel has stopped playing with words. He has acquired the habit of important things. His address is there. He is living in Orlando and has just been granted political asylum. He promised to tell me all about it, but I can imagine what he had to go through, poor thing. I will take the letter with me.

It was Jeannot who brought it. He dropped in to see me. He looked odd in his woollen jacket. I had never seen him in that get-up. I never liked him anyway. He is a prickly character who spends his life between flights. Officially he is in import-export. I am not the only one who thinks he has his little deals on the side. He once told me that the Head of Customs had denounced him in some high and obscure quarter. He got a summons from the President himself. At nine o'clock at night, in his office at the palace. He went. He knew that running away was not the answer. The President asked him if he imported arms in his containers. He said no, but made it clear that he could do so if that would be

95

of service to the Revolution. He left the palace with the President's private telephone numbers. He brags about using them against the Head of Customs when he behaved as if he had forgotten that he, Jeannot, had been into the snake pit without getting bitten.

He came in wearing his jacket and left it behind. As he went out he said to me:

"You'll be needing it. But first you'd better take something of yours from the inside pocket."

It was the letter from Fresnel. It is now safe with the ones that took me three days to find. I can imagine my cousin's face if he had found these letters.

I sold my shop. I needed to make my story move faster. In my family, you die in your shop. If everything is going well. But it isn't. My cousin took over the shop. We spent a night discussing the consequences of my decision. He didn't understand a thing. For over a century we have buried ourselves in the trivialisation of events. This country has created a complex system of short cuts for itself, to keep the dysfunction functioning. I have stopped feeding the utopia. In a week I am leaving.

I will take the time for a walk round the town. Before I go I would like to know who is going to make it their business to liberate the day. I will take whatever time I need to make my fear waver. I have time. No one is expecting me for a week. I would never have imagined that one day passion would show me the way to the dawn. It is not the night. You never go out during the night to come back during the night. Let's hope this week and what it holds doesn't try to stop what is forging ahead. In all honesty, I am on the downward slope to exile. It's better that way. I need to take a step back to be able to understand what was once my country.

14

HERE WE ARE. In a few days' time it is the Festival of the Revolution. Port-au-Prince is getting ready to change its image. This festival is a rag-bag in praise of the President. Those who have never taken part or been subjected to the parade have obviously not set foot in the capital of Haiti. Photos of the smiling leader will face up to gusts of wind, opponents and the dust in the street. People who have never been near the town on a day of kow-towing to the reign of the night can never imagine the weight of the presidential sash.

The procession always sets off from the cathedral, makes its way through the rows of choirboys with the blessing of the Apostolic Nuncio and His Holiness the Archbishop, both gleaming in suitable robes. Outside, in broad daylight, pupils from the Convent schools stand in front of those from the State schools, waving cut-out coloured paper flags in their privileged little hands. The crowd, which comes from everywhere, greets the procession with "Long live the President!"

Farmers, workers, recycled poor people, women, all throw themselves at His Excellency's imposing personal body-guard. The good thing is that it is always the same ones who have done this show for years. Gently, the guards hold back the good people, making sure to let some slip through to be greeted by the President. They will not give up until the

President invites two or three of them to get into his car; the people's car, he will later call it.

This year I have been invited to the palace. It was Zaccharias who arranged for me to have a place of honour. Third row. Behind the foreign diplomats. I will be three rows in front of the other Jews and a thousand miles from the people. It is a shopkeeper's duty to appear in the palace courtyard at the festival. It is also the change we get from our contributions to the special festival fund. Zaccharias numbers me among his friends. But he doesn't know that Fresnel has written to me. He is alive. He is waiting for me in Miami.

I will not go to this party in honour of the President. I will not wear the badge worn by his henchmen. I say this with all my soul, annoyed by the night. The cries beneath my window, the news, the faces ravaged by complicit mornings have got the better of my innate sense of collaboration.

It is a long time since I stopped dreaming about being a historian or a politician. Let the street deck itself out with guests on the big day, let the cars blow their horns til my eardrums burst. I will not carry the flag of the night during the daytime. All year round the people hide themselves away. At every carnival they are brought out with a roll of drums. At every anniversary of the Revolution they are brought out with a lot of popular hogwash and promises. The street is getting ready to be full of life, hostage to merchants of death wearing full regalia. Even in this country of days at half-mast, the sun still manages to play along.

Although I am a Jew, I will not give a cent towards the next campaign. The weapons bought with my contribution and that of so many others are always turned on us, on our secrets. The army's new anti-riot company might be well trained and reassuring, but I am not going to see it. I left the good old days of naivety and principles at the last crossroads. We have always paid for the right to live in the semblance of a country. Our shops and our origins have always doomed us to collaborate, to serve both God and Caesar.

This is my country no longer. The radio gets on my nerves. The official communiqués make my life a misery. They always have to put salt on dried blood. As if fresh blood lived on confessions. It is a country that is always apologising. Too many contrasts. They throw a party to celebrate last night's harvest. This country is sinking into another country, with its hundreds of thousands of children waiting for death in the capital alone. Life is leaving, moving far away from love, far away from freedom. I am going with it.

This year I am not going to listen to the same old speech that I have heard for the last ten years.

"I am proud to be the worthy successor of Toussaint-Louverture and Dessalines the Great. I assume the responsibility of leading the Haitian people on the road to progress and democracy. How many of my brothers and sisters, here and elsewhere, do not believe in the Haitian miracle? And I reply with all my strength that our ancestors routed Napoleon's army at the cost of many sacrifices and that our generation will repeat this achievement. Not with weapons, but with our industries, our roads and our agriculture. History requires us to defend our status of being an example to other black peoples. With the international community, hand in hand with our friends from industry and commerce, together with the enlightened opposition, my team and I pledge to honour the solemn promises we made before the people when we accepted the mandate to secure the future of this country in order and discipline."

By the time the band at the National Palace strikes up the first verse I will be on the plane, en route to the madness of another life. Out of the window I will see the distance between this people and the others. I am not going to wait for night before I leave. I am afraid its reign will threaten my meagre right to escape.

PART THREE

THIS IS FRESNEL'S LETTER to Jeremy Assaël. I will keep it for as long as my journey lasts.

Jeremy,

I am writing to you from the balcony of my apartment. It is a beautiful day. People are happy. At least they look happy. If I dare to sit in a deckchair and show myself to my neighbours, it is because as from this morning I am an official asylum-seeker with the right to live with Uncle Sam. I get an allowance from the State of Florida which will give me something to live on during the time it takes me to integrate. My immediate project is you. Then I am going to write a book, a novel that will talk about exile and crossings. I must write it in English, otherwise it will never see the light of day.

I think it is important that you think about shutting up shop. If I was allowed to make decisions for you, you would already be in the United States, the Dominican Republic, anywhere, making a new life for yourself. On the other hand I am keen to tell you about my departure, to explain why I believe your future in Haiti is engraved with mourning.

6th October

I was at the private viewing of Pascal's exhibition. I introduced him to you once at Kenskoff. He is a young painter whose theme is naked creatures displaying their genitals. Feeling a need to support his creative talent in the face of nostalgic and caustic critics, I made it my duty to be with him for this venture.

Disastrous evening. The management smothered the art. It is good to see an artist friend's work take off, but I can tell you the way it was done left us speechless. Pascal's paintings were wildly successful, out of all proportion. Madame Célestin, the gallery owner, had set up an incredible marketing strategy to get her own back on the press, who had refused to publicise the event. It was amazing. Using her connections at the National Palace, she managed to get one of Pascal's pictures hung in the President's office. Ministers saw it. Diplomats liked it. Collectors got wind of a bargain. You can imagine the stampede for poor Pascal's canvases. Within half an hour they were all reserved. Sold.

More disgusted than pleased, the barely-known artist managed to slip away from the pack of de facto *connoisseurs and join me at the Café des Arts. I had arranged this refuge in case we needed to beat a retreat. It was the only way of avoiding a drama, because I had a desperate urge to burst out laughing, the scene was so unreal and foolish.*

Almost 10 p m

Particularly cool evening. Pascal was doing his best to spend his old pennies. He had to make room for tomorrow's jackpot. He is a Third World artist. Money hampers his necessity to create. The sooner the money is spent the better. I know instinctively that it is the crappiest situations that drive an artist to the limits of his relentless struggle to transform and create. It is the wretchedness of Haiti that produces so many artists and pocket politicians.

A waiter brought us a bottle of champagne which we had not ordered. I was just explaining to him that he must have got the wrong table when a deluxe creature planted herself in front of me and demanded a gift fit for a queen. She invited us to share the bottle with her. Aside from the impossibility of refusing her, she was genuinely interested in Pascal's work. The emptier the bottle became, the more she insisted on posing for a portrait by Pascal. Flattered, my dear artist friend agreed. They left me with the remains of the bottle and went off to get to know each other better, far from me, far from the noise.

I don't know what stars they lit up together. I had a bottle to finish and a vague plan to go home. I didn't get time. They didn't give me time.

Rather too late I noticed the terrace of the café had emptied like a spendthrift's wallet. I found myself surrounded by the last remaining customers. They were armed and determined to take me away. They had had the order to do it.

I have always compared my country to a big open stage. That's simply my belief. It's true that everyday life always contains elements of the carnival; but the facts, which I forget too quickly, were overwhelming. The unusual aspect of the story had overshadowed my fear. I was wrong to interpret what was happening as imaginary. The guys in front of me really did have something against me. Their boss had decided on it.

I promise you I hadn't spent all day thinking about death or prison. When at the start of the evening I saw Pascal's pictures selling, I caught myself dreaming about an idle future. I even believed that art could set itself up as a sideline in this country that has lost the power of speech.

Even in my hazy state, the infernal machine had got underway. These henchmen were not interested in playing games. They were there to take me away. You understand, Jeremy. It was what they were used to. And I didn't feel at all scared. I held out my wrists to them, one last request for civilised treatment. I wanted to have real handcuffs for the honour of being arrested with dignity. Like every Haitian, I had often imagined how I would react if I was arrested. I had vowed I would ask to be treated as a delinquent, a common-law criminal. In a country where a crust of bread is worth as much a human being, it is wiser to go to prison labelled as a criminal than as an opponent of the government.

The poor henchmen did not have any handcuffs. Since I put up no resistance, they had to make do with taking me away. The journey to my cell was quite comfortable. The night that accompanied me had already vacuumed up any citizens without a badge, without an official permit to be out on the street. Flanked by two militants, guardians of the Revolution, I just let myself be taken to meet the silence. In these circumstances, words would only bounce off the walls of propaganda. I think all Haitians are disappointed. I searched the faces of my abductors. I had the time. I don't think they enjoyed spying on the shadows of the night either. I imagined them doing another job apart from this. The one on my left would make a good farmer, I'm sure. The one on the right was a young guy, well-hung. He would be good as a chulo*, looking after tourists who are recovering from heartbreak.*

As long as you are still living in Haiti, I will refrain from telling you what I was subjected to during my interrogation. I didn't get the chance to see my torturer's face, but I think I know who it was. His voice was already all round town by way of rumour and half-hearted attempts at revolt. He questioned me in a broken French to which only His Lordship has the key. His normal way of speaking, resumed whenever he laughed, has livened up so many evenings that I couldn't not put a name to his voice. Our discussion centred on the woman who had gone off with Pascal. It turned out she was the ex-companion of one of the regime's musclemen. This man could not stand having his honour dragged through the paintings of some dauber who had struck lucky. I was accused of being an accomplice to the kidnapping of this woman. I swear to you she went with Pascal of her own free will, that I had absolutely no idea where they were going or what they were planning to do.

I can still remember the fiery notes of that night. But I will never be able to forget the risk that the young man who was on my right in the car took to save my life.

After an interrogation that made liberal use of torture, the spare lackeys had to drive me to a safe place. In my case it was safe conduct to some obscure spot outside the town. It's simpler that way. It saves any gawkers in town from spitting on one more corpse, one death too many.

---

* Dandy.

When the car pulled up I thought my last moment had come. The young man with the face of a chulo *took me by the hand and motioned me to get out.*

"Mr Fresnel sir, I was in your history class at the lycée. *I don't remember a whole lot of it. But you told us about nights like this which punctuate the history of our people. I don't believe in this Revolution any more, which forces me to work as a killer. One more death is hardly going to do the government any good. I suggest you get out and seek refuge in the Dominican Republic. I know someone who can help you get across the border. He lives just opposite from here. He'll know what to do. Don't worry about us. No one is going to check that there is one more body on the mass grave at Titanyen*. I can count on my allies. We all have our moments of weakness. It's our way of believing in this country. Don't thank me. The bosses are nice and warm at home. Too scared to go out. So we've given ourselves the pleasure of having the right of reprieve. Haiti is a crazy country which spins round and round. When it stops it's never in the same place."*

Calmly, the smuggler took me back to my house to pick up my papers. Then he took me into the next-door Republic. We celebrated with Dominican soldiers until daybreak. It was the first time in my life that I had left Haiti without intending to return. Afterwards I was able to leave for the United States.

Now, let's talk about you.

Jeremy, I know you well enough to imagine your state of mind. You think you are vested with the power of continuity. That's not true. Your family has its secrets and has always revealed them in the form of symbolic references. You were born in a shop and you have always lived for that shop. Far from envying your situation, I think you were duped by a strict system. You are just a pawn in a history that has been reshaped to fit.

---

* Town to the north of Port-au-Prince.

Unintentionally, your grandparents were players in a grand political manoeuvre. By the last quarter of the nineteenth century, the French had given up the idea of regaining their sometime pearl of the West Indies. Haitian independence was already spent; all the more so as the general abolition of slavery had won over the intellectuals and the workers. Meanwhile, the Germans, Italians and other Europeans were imposing their way of life on America and the Caribbean. So the old mother country killed two birds with one stone. On the one hand, it rid itself of its motley population of Sephardic Jews, Lebanese, Syrians and Palestinians who had previously washed up on the Mediterranean coastline. France had other plans for the sunny coastal regions. They had to make sure there was enough room for areas with plenty of villas, and that little Marseilles did not spring up everywhere along the coast. And on the other hand, this policy let France get its revenge on Haiti by forcing them to take their surplus immigrants.

An agreement between the two countries allowed the first Levantines to settle in Haiti. They got quite a warm reception. After all, they were professionals who were useful to the country's moribund economy. Once the floodgates opened, the number of arrivals increased at an alarming rate. And it was no longer professionals, but mostly down-and-outs who wanted to get themselves a place in the sun by fair means or foul. The Haitian government were not slow to react. They quickly retracted, although some observers said it was too late.

The people of Haiti did not look favourably on the new settlers. A clash of cultures? The Levantines ran local shops. Informal trade. They took their cheap wares to the remotest parts of the country and made a small fortune out of them. Imagine it now, foreigners in strange get-up wandering round the streets, busy ruining you by offering illicit goods to your customers. Jeremy, I'm sure you would be the first to the barricades. I don't want to make any judgement on your people's past, on your class, but you ought to know that this has never been your country. What's more, with all the money you have made, the day will come when you are going to have some explaining to do. If you have the time, of course.

It has already been said that the Haitian lives locked away inside a theatrical performance. I am Haitian and I accept this caricature. There is also the carnival and the Mardi Gras. This day marks the end of the festival, of the madness. It is the day when the victims dare to confront their torturers and/or their descendants. Every year there is a procession of the condemned: the policeman, the colonist, the American invader, the Protestant pastor, the Catholic priest, the politician, the intellectual, the banker, the big landowner, the Dominican whore, the flea-bitten artist, the wandering Jew.

Every year, when it comes to burying the masks, all the fires are presented with the wandering Jew. Always the wandering Jew, every Mardi Gras. Remember you are a wandering Jew and that your place is on the road.